Brian Delahunt

T·H·E

DETECTIVE'S MUSE

A Niall O'Huiginn Mystery

This is a work of fiction. Names, characters, places and incidents either are the product of the author's imagination or are used fictitiously, and any resemblance to any actual persons, living or dead, events, or locales is entirely coincidental.

Printed in the United States of America

ISBN: 0-982-70150-0
ISBN-13: 9780982701508
Library of Congress Control Number: 2010909454

Spider Bite Press
Greenbrae, California

For Mom, Dad, Nancy and Stephanie

PROLOGUE

Anne Tadmore knew she shouldn't be here. Why had she surrendered to her obsession? Random bursts from her nervous system created a tic in her right eye. She laughed nervously, but she had to know if Martin was seeing someone else. She mounted the three brick steps in front of Martin's house, stopped to take a deep breath, and then rang the bell.

There was no response, so she pushed it again. After waiting several seconds she headed to the backyard to retrieve the hidden key. Anne walked alongside the house, and stopped to look in each window. She cupped her eyes and pressed her head against the cold glass, but the inside was dark.

When she reached the hiding spot, she removed her black leather gloves, and picked up the small stone Buddha that Martin had brought back from India on one of his many trips.

Anne shivered but couldn't tell if it was the anticipation or the cold winter wind. She shook the Buddha and the house keys dropped into her palm. She bounced them in her hand a few times as she approached the back door, then knocked. No response.

She turned the key in the lock, and the door swung open.

Martin hadn't returned any of her calls even though she'd been leaving him messages for two days. Anne paused in the doorway to listen, tilted her head and sniffed the air like a wary animal searching for the presence of danger. The escaping warm air carried several odors: rotting garbage, spices, tea, and cat food. The combination made her eyes water.

Martin didn't leave his house smelly. He hated dirt. Something was wrong, very wrong.

Under the sounds of the whistling wind and the bare tree branches creaking, she detected a faint vibration. Anne strained to block out the exterior sounds, then took a step into the kitchen and listened again. No question about it. A scratching echoed from somewhere inside.

"Harry," she called quietly.

The cat didn't answer but the scratching grew in urgency. Anne reassured herself that Martin's cat had gotten stuck in one of the rooms and wanted out.

"Martin," she called, louder. It wasn't like him not to phone when he promised. "Harry," she called again.

The scratching sound grew more intense each time she called. She rubbed her right eye in a vain attempt to quell the tic.

The light switch was on the opposite side of the room; Martin called it a design flaw. When she stepped between the table and the counter, her running shoes met an unexpected obstacle. She jumped back, bumped into the door, and pressed herself against it.

"Shit! Damn!" she muttered.

Still no sounds except the scratching and her heavy breathing. She tried to make out the object on the floor, but the only light was the flashing red on the answering machine on the counter.

She could leave right now. Put the key back, return to her warm house, and nobody would ever know she'd been here.

"What am I doing here anyway?" Anne knew the answer: Her life was out of control.

She continued to stand in the dark kitchen of the man who had rejected her, on several occasions, but couldn't take her eyes off the black object in the middle of the floor. Could it be Martin lying there? Her stomach knotted, and the scratching continued. Coming to Martin's house didn't seem like such a good idea anymore; it felt more like another step into her own hell.

She set out for the other side of the kitchen, keeping her eyes glued to the object on the floor. The closer she drew the less it looked like Martin – or anybody else. She had studied him often enough over the last few years, but to be certain she would have to move closer. Anne squatted, extended her and touched it. The object gave under the pressure of her index finger. It felt familiar which permitted her to explore the surface.

She stepped over the bundle, walked directly to the light switch and flipped it.

In the middle of the floor two fifty-pound bags of tea lay end to end. He must have just received a shipment, she thought.

Anne glanced at the answering machine on the kitchen counter. *Should I erase all my messages?*

The continuous scratching sound began to frighten her, but the fear quickly became a rush of anger. She pushed open the door to the dining room. The sound was clearer now. Anne hesitated only a second before plunging into the room. She crossed the dining room registering only that the table was set for two, and went into the living room. The sound seemed louder. She realized the scratching originated in the bedroom.

Anne moved toward the bedroom door. Harry lay curled into a ball on the couch and a familiar suitcase rested by the front door. If Harry was in the living room, who or what was scratching beyond the closed bedroom door? Anne stopped, a wave of nausea rising inside her.

"Martin, it's Anne. Is that you?"

She forced herself to move and push open the bedroom door. The frantic pace of the scratching increased. The noise came from behind the closet door.

Her stomach tightened even more. Anne hesitated, took a deep breath, turned on the light, then walked to the closet door. She needed to know.

She covered her mouth with the palm of her left hand and grasped the doorknob with her right hand. A bead of sweat traced down her back between her shoulder blades and her goosebumps.

Anne pulled open the door and jumped back in one fluid movement, ready for whatever.

But not for what she saw.

Under the neatly hung suits, shirts, and pants a naked woman sat, bound and gagged. The woman stared at Anne with tears streaming down her face. Her forehead was raw from rubbing against the door, and blood spotted her face. The woman looked familiar. Anne focused.

"Oh! Sara," was all she could say.

Her hands shook, from anger or fear. Anne wanted to vomit, but she forced herself to pull Sara from the closet. The gag came off easily; Sara sucked in long deep breaths. The bindings on her hands and feet took longer to remove. Anne struggled with untying the strips of towel. Both women cried, for different reasons. Sara couldn't straighten her legs, and Anne helped rub the life back into them until she was able to get to her feet. Sara stumbled on her weak legs and whispered a weak "thank you" to Anne.

Anne didn't know what to say to her best friend and business partner. Her head felt like it was going to explode. Finally, unable to control herself or bear the silence between them she said, "Where's Martin?"

"Gone. They must have taken him."

* * *

CHAPTER I

Lieutenant Niall O'Huiginn turned away from the death reports and the pile of 1998 year-end statistics that he had to finish by Monday. He studied an icicle glimmering outside the window of his basement office. The crystalline dagger had formed soon after the cold front moved into Hilltop, New Jersey, and he wondered how long it would hang there before it, too, disappeared from his life. He spun his chair around and marked his calendar, then realized he might not remember why he'd made the mark; he decided to add 'icicle'.

His cell phone rang in the pocket of his coat hanging across the room, and he sat for a long second staring blankly in that direction. He'd bought the bulky phone so Maggie could call whenever she needed him but she'd died on his birthday a year ago last October. Why hadn't he set the voicemail to pickup? Perhaps a miracle would happen and it would be her at the other end. He shook the thoughts out of his head. Maggie was gone and that was that.

Only his mother would let the phone ring and ring without seeming to care if he ever answered. Niall walked around his desk and got the still-ringing phone from the inside pocket of his heavy woolen coat.

"Hi, Mama."

"How in the name of God did you know it was me?"

"Who else would let a phone ring for five minutes?"

"Don't be fresh," she said. "It was that long, was it?"

"It was." Perhaps that was an exaggeration, but he was certain she would have let it continue to ring until he answered.

Her voice sounded so clear it was hard to believe she was in the west of Ireland. Niall pictured her keeping warm by the peat stove.

"Well, why didn't you answer it sooner?"

"I was busy." He returned to his swivel chair, put his feet on the desk and watched the lone icicle glimmering.

"What are you so busy doing that you can't stop to talk to me, and how is it I haven't heard from you in three weeks?" When Niall didn't reply her tone softened and she asked in Irish, "Cad é ata cearr a ghrá?" She always switched to Irish when she was serious. She had called him either 'a ghrá' (my love) or Niall og (young Niall) all his life.

"Nothing's wrong. I have a lot of year-end paperwork to finish."

"Don't be talking nonsense. I'm your mother. You should have come to see us for Christmas, Niall og. It wasn't good for you to stay alone. Did you forget we were alone in America when your father died, God rest his soul?"

He remained silent.

"I know what you went through but she passed away more than a year ago. You have to get on with your life."

"It's not because of Maggie, Mom. I just have a lot of paper work at this time of year." Niall didn't like lying to his mother. She was right but he just couldn't let go.

"You're a handsome man, and it won't do you or anyone else a bit of good if your beautiful sandy hair turns gray with worry. Maggie told you she didn't want you pining away, didn't she?"

Niall didn't respond.

"Are you going to answer me?"

"Yes, I remember what she said." He continued staring at the icicle.

"And you're only 37 years young, aren't you?"

"Yes." It was better not to incite her further.

"God help you if I have to come back to America to straighten you out, and you know I will, don't you?"

"Yes, I do, but I'm fine, Mom. Really, I'm fine."

He caught a movement out of the corner of his eye and turned. Mettler was filling the doorway with his six-foot five-inch, 275-pound body.

"Listen, Mom. Anthony just arrived. He needs me. I have to go. How's everything with you and Ciarán?"

"We're well. You'll call me, of course."

"I'll call you next weekend. Tell Ciarán I'll call him soon, too. I'm glad you called, Mom." This time he wasn't lying.

"Goodbye Niall og, and say hello to Anthony for me."

"I will, indeed."

Niall shut off the phone and motioned for Mettler to enter.

"Sorry to disturb your call to your mother, sir, but we just received a report of a woman found tied up in a closet. She's alive but weak. Apparently, she'd been in there for a couple of days before she was found. Do you want me to send Herzog, or should I go?"

Niall glanced at the pile of work he had to do, then back at Sergeant Anthony Mettler. The youthful thirty-year-old Mettler rubbed the top of his military-style haircut as he waited for a response.

"Who's there now?" Niall asked.

"Sergeant Boehm is at the house. He requested detectives."

Niall looked at the pile of folders on his desk again.

"No, I'll go. You finish these two death reports." He pushed the papers toward Mettler. "Leave them on my desk, and then go home. I'll sign them in the morning."

"Are you sure that's wise, sir."

"I trust you to finish the reports properly and, besides, it will be good training for when you get my job."

"No sir, I meant is it wise for you to go alone. You know, without me." He hesitated. "Because of what happened last time."

Niall had to maneuver his way around Mettler to retrieve his coat. He felt dwarfed next to him, even though he was six feet and 180 pounds.

"What's the address?" He asked irritated.

Did he need or want Mettler along? Yes, he'd taken a few risks after Maggie died but he was over it. Mettler mothered him. At first, he welcomed his sympathy and concern but it never ended. Now he found himself part of every Mettler family celebration, whether it was a birthday party or the contrived New Year's barbecue his wife had concocted to introduce Niall to a girlfriend from work.

"3636 Claremont Avenue," Mettler said.

"O.K., let's go. You'll still have to do the reports."

"Yes sir, no problem."

* * *

CHAPTER II

There were two patrol units and an ambulance in front of the single-story, brick-fronted house. Mettler went directly inside while Niall studied the area.

This was one of the better neighborhoods. Niall glanced up and down the avenue. The area was silent except for the creaking of bare branches. Freeze-dried Christmas trees sat at the curb waiting to be hauled away, and colorful holiday lights still flickered on houses.

There were no people in the street. Usually, the red flashing lights attracted crowds, but the frigid night had kept even the most curious indoors; a few neighbors were observing the scene from the warmth behind their double-pane windows.

He pulled his coat closed, then walked up the clean concrete pathway that split the small lawn leading to the front door. All the lights in the house blazed. A row of manicured evergreen bushes on either side of the entrance stood under new storm windows and a pristine glass storm door protected the freshly painted front door.

Niall stepped into the house's living room, closing the door behind him. An expensive-looking oriental rug carpeted the 10-by-12-foot room to a hallway across from him. Sergeants Boehm and

Mettler were huddled in front of an open door at the end of the hallway. A calico cat slept on a black leather couch to his left. A faint spicy odor reminded him of an Indian restaurant and seemed a part of the house. The immaculately clean interior was devoid of any frills; it was a man's house.

The dining room through an archway opening was on his right. Niall guessed that the swinging door on the left wall of the dining room led to the kitchen. He ambled into the dining room to study the scene. The table was set for two, with crystal wine and water glasses, china plates, silver utensils, and linen napkins. An unopened bottle of red wine and a corkscrew sat between the two place settings. Looks like a romantic dinner that never happened.

The arrangement was neat and precise, like everything he'd seen so far. There wasn't even any dust on the dark dining room furniture. Niall thought that his mother would like the cleanliness of the place, but not the smell.

He heard raised angry voices from the kitchen, and recognized Officer Deborah Flemming's tone. She'd been on the force for three years, but he'd had only passing contact with her. She was young, full of drive, and out to prove herself. She was a martial arts buff. Niall had heard other people say that she had too much testosterone.

When he pushed open the door, the scent of spices was much heavier and the air sparkled with tension. Flemming and an attractive young woman stood almost nose-to-nose, screeching at each other.

"It's none of your business what I did or didn't do," the young woman said to Flemming.

Flemming was pointing her finger at the woman's face when she realized someone else had entered. She dropped her finger.

"Hello, sir," she said.

Her thick black hair had grown below her shoulders since Niall had last seen her. She looked softer and more feminine than he remembered.

"Greetings, Flemming. I thought you were on vacation."

"Ah, no sir, I returned last week."

"Are we having a problem in here?"

"NO SIR, not at all."

"Good. And who might you be?" He asked the other woman, whose face was red with anger.

Flemming replied, "This is Anne Tadmore, Lieutenant. She's the one who found Sara Collins in the closet and had her take a shower, probably destroying evidence."

"Thank you, Flemming. I'll take over. Go outside and make sure that traffic doesn't get congested behind our vehicles."

Flemming sputtered but obeyed. The door swung several times after she left the room.

"Don't let the door hit you on the way out, Officer Flemming," Anne Tadmore called.

Tadmore looked to be in her mid- to late-twenties. She wore a bulky green down parka, pressed jeans, and white tennis shoes. She stood with her arms crossed tightly.

Her attitude perplexed Niall. He couldn't discern the reason for her protective stance but didn't think it was just anger.

Anne Tadmore. Her name struck a familiar chord. Did he know her? Then it dawned on him. An t-adh mór. It was Irish for good luck.

He inspected the small kitchen to allow her time to calm down. The room was even neater and cleaner than the rest of the house. There weren't any pots or pans on the stove or counters.

A large collection of spice and herb jars was arranged in alphabetical order on the countertop next to the stove.

"I apologize if officer Flemming was out of line with you. Please, sit at the table here and tell me what happened this evening."

Niall pulled out a chair for her at the rectangular farmhouse style table and sat down opposite her. Tadmore placed her hands flat on the table. Off-white paint covered her cuticles. When she noticed him looking at her hands, she tucked them under her arms. The rosy glow on her cheeks had diminished, but the glazed look of shock remained in her beautiful green eyes. She had short red-brown hair. Her ears almost looked pointy, and for a second she reminded him of a spéirbean, a fairy woman, from the stories his father and uncle had told him. He could not help wondering what the rest of her looked like under the massive coat.

"Why are you looking at me that way, and who are you anyway?"

"Excuse me. I'm Lieutenant O'Huiginn. I didn't mean to make you uncomfortable. It's just that you reminded me of something."

"It must have been a nightmare."

Niall smiled. She did not know how close she was to the truth. The dreams he had about his father's death and the constant repetition of his unfinished aisling poem had haunted him since childhood.

"I'd like you to tell me what happened here this evening."

She shifted, but remained silent.

"I'm not here to judge you or anyone else. I only want to find whoever did such a terrible thing to Miss Collins. It is Miss Collins, isn't it?"

Again she did not answer, but Niall saw pain in her glowing green gaze. Was it because of her friend?

"Stay here and try to relax. I'm going to see how your friend is feeling. I'll send someone to keep you company." He stood to leave.

"I'd prefer to be alone."

"It might be better if you had other people around you for the moment."

"Don't send that woman cop."

"I wouldn't dream of doing such a thing to you." Niall smiled. He again studied the place settings on the dining room table. Who was supposed to have dinner here? A photo of a man on the opposite wall grabbed his attention and h e walked toward it.

Mettler appeared in the doorway and broke his concentration. "Ah, there you are, sir. They're about to take Ms. Collins to the hospital for observation and a full examination. It seems that –."

Niall silenced him with a motion. "Let's talk over there." After they moved to the front door, he said, "Go ahead. Tell me about it."

"Ms. Collins is dehydrated, and they gave her something to calm her nerves, which also loosened her tongue. She told me that she and Ms. Tadmore are like sisters. Her father became Ms. Tadmore's guardian after her parents died. They live together and work together painting houses –."

"And it looks like they share the same men."

"How'd you know that, sir?"

"Mostly speculation," Niall admitted. "And how many times do I have to tell you to call me Niall? We've worked together for four years."

"Right, sir."

They'd had the same conversation a hundred times and Mettler still refused to call him Niall. At times, Mettler reminded him of a character from a BBC mystery more than a New Jersey cop.

"What else did she say?"

"Ms. Tadmore had it bad for this guy, Martin Charon." He glanced at his notes. "They painted his house two years ago and became friends. They've stayed close. Ms. Tadmore wanted more from him but Charon has kept her at bay with empty promises. Then a week or two ago he started hitting on Ms. Collins and convinced her to spend some time with him. On Wednesday, Ms. Collins told Ms. Tadmore she was going to visit friends in Washington, D.C. for three days, but instead she came over here."

"Nothing like lifelong friendship."

"Right, sir. Anyway, that night the doorbell rang while they were playing house," Mettler continued. "Ms. Collins hid in the kitchen just in case it might be Ms. Tadmore but it was two Indian guys, from India, and they started arguing with Charon. Then the three of them switched from English to Hindi, and Ms. Collins couldn't understand anything. The men continued to argue and she heard them coming toward the kitchen. Before she could move, the door flew open and she was knocked backwards. She remembers losing her balance, falling backwards, and then nothing until she came to, tied up and naked in the closet. She didn't hear any sounds until Ms. Tadmore came in the back door a little over an hour ago. Ms. Collins banged her forehead so hard on the closet door to attract attention that she cut it."

"Was she able to remember any of what they said in English?"

"I barely got this much out of her."

Niall frowned. "There's something else going on here with this group, I feel it. It's right in front of my eyes but I can't see it. Did you find anything out about Martin Charon yet?"

"Only that he's a professor of mid-east studies at the university, and that his car is still in the garage."

"Put his name out on the radio, and then start wrapping it up. I'm going back to talk to Miss Tadmore to see if she's ready to add anything to the picture. We'll have a long talk with Miss Collins tomorrow, when hopefully she'll be able to remember what they said."

He pushed open the swinging door and saw Anne Tadmore standing at the far wall staring into the kitchen pantry. She looked perplexed.

"Did you lose something?"

"Ah, no, I just thought it might be nice to have a cup of tea. Martin imports tea on the side, and he always has a good supply."

Niall didn't believe her. "Really, I'm surprised he has time for that."

Tadmore's forehead creased. She pulled her coat closed again.

"Come over, and sit down again so we can finish. What else can you tell me about Mr. Charon?" Niall asked gently.

"What do you want to know?" she asked dropping into the chair again.

"What prompted you to come here tonight?"

"I thought something might be wrong." She twisted her short hair with an index finger.

"What gave you that idea?"

"I was supposed to meet Martin for an early dinner tonight..."

"Excuse me, but what about Miss Collins? Was she invited to dinner too?"

She dropped her hand to her lap and her face flushed. "No," she said in a controlled voice. "Sara was supposed to be home late this afternoon. I was a little concerned when I hadn't heard from her but I figured she was having a good time. Besides, things between us have been tense for a few weeks, and I needed some alone time to recharge my battery. Now I understand why she was so touchy."

"Thanks. Please continue. You were supposed to meet Martin for dinner?"

"Yes, that's right. I hadn't heard from him for several days, so I called this morning to confirm time and place, but he never called back, which isn't like him. He's sickeningly punctual."

"What kind of dinner was it?"

"We're friends. Friends go out to eat sometimes. Don't you have friends?"

"Relax. I'm just trying to find out what happened to your friends." Niall held up his hands in surrender. "Martin is very neat, isn't he?"

"I think it has to do with his background. He grew up in India."

"Do you know anybody who'd want to do him harm, Miss Tadmore?"

"I'd do him harm if I got my hands on him and call me, Anne."

"Well then, Anne, what can you tell me about Martin Charon?"

"He teaches Eastern studies and Hindi at the university. He has two PhDs."

Niall thought he was supposed to be impressed so he leaned toward her to show interest. "He must be very intelligent."

"I thought he was until… Anyway, like I said, he was born in India where his father worked for a large multinational company. Martin grew up with an Indian nanny and learned Hindi almost before English. He also learned to love tea when he was little. His parents moved back here when he was twelve, but he never lost his interest in the language and the culture. I guess that's why he specialized in it at school. Now he teaches, runs student tours during the summer, and imports tea."

"Professor Charon seems quite versatile," Niall observed, but Anne had stopped talking. "Thank you. I have one or two more questions, and then you can leave."

"What more do you want to know?" She pulled her coat tightly around her again.

"I'd like to know how you got into the house and what transpired after you entered."

He pushed his chair back from the table and crossed his legs, figuring if he looked relaxed, she might relax enough to open up to him, but minutes passed without her saying anything. It had been a long day and he was tired. Sara Collins' statement had confirmed what he suspected about the trio, but why was she left in the closet? It didn't feel like something Charon would do; the house was too neat. Charon's life was too neat. Had the two Indian men put Collins in the closet? Why would they undress her? Was she raped? Where was Martin Charon?

The door swung open and banged against the counter.

"Sorry, sir. I didn't realize I used that much force." Mettler looked from Niall to Anne Tadmore and back again. He started to say something else, then stopped.

"No, it's all right. We're finished here for the moment. The rest of our questions can wait until tomorrow. OK, Anne?" Niall smiled at her.

Mettler said, "They're taking Ms. Collins to the hospital, but she wants to have a word with Ms. Tadmore first."

Tadmore didn't appear thrilled by the prospect. "Escort Anne to her friend. I'll be along in a moment."

Anne left with Mettler.

Niall envisioned Sara Collins standing on this side of the door when the door flew open. He crouched down and checked the table and the floor for signs of blood. The leg of the table looked like it had been scrubbed and the smell of lemon oil reached his nostrils. Charon had cleaned the table before they left. The floor was spotless too. The guy was definitely a neat freak.

Where was he?

* * *

CHAPTER III

They were lifting Sara Collins into the ambulance as he walked outside. Niall hung back for a second, then walked toward Anne. The vehicle pulled away, and he heard her mumble, "Bitch."

"Did you drive here?" he asked.

She sucked in a deep breath and stepped back. "No, I walked."

"It's way too cold for you to walk home. Wait one moment while I give a few instructions to the officers, then I'll drive you."

"What have I got to lose?" Her shoulders sagged. She dropped her glance to the cold ground.

Niall went to the bedroom and looked around. The bed was a mess and Sara Collin's clothes were thrown in the far corner. Although, the closet door where she'd spent the last few days was closed, the room smelled fetid, far from the antiseptic quality of the rest of the house. Would Charon clean the table where Sara Collins had hit her head but leave the bedroom in this condition? That didn't make any sense.

"Were there any signs of a break-in, Anthony?"

"No, sir. The windows and doors are all clean."

"Why do you think this room is such a mess while the rest of the house is spotless?"

"I don't know, sir. Maybe he didn't have time to clean or was in a real hurry to leave."

"Maybe, but I doubt it. I'm driving Anne Tadmore home. Finish here and make sure the house is sealed. I'll see you in the morning. If we're lucky, they'll find Charon before then."

Niall stopped to look at Charon's office where diplomas, letters of congratulations, and pictures adorned the off-white walls, all hung at the same level. A leather chair, an oak roll-top desk with a lamp and phone on it, two bookcases, and a dark red carpet rounded out the décor. He ran a finger along a bookshelf, no dust. Martin Charon was in all the photos most of which were with women.

An eight-by-eleven picture on the desk was autographed in a flowing style: Martin Todd Charon. Niall laughed and lifted it, could the fella be that full of himself? It was an old-fashioned black and white photo that reminded him of the movie stars from the 1930s. Charon was thin with long dark brown hair, not bad-looking but also nothing out of the ordinary. Niall took the photo with him to have copies made to hand out to the uniforms.

He walked back outside. Anne Tadmore stood alone in the cold, moving back and forth to keep warm. Flemming stood by the squad cars flapping her arms to keep warm and waiting to direct a car if one happened to come down the street.

"Sorry I took so long. I hope you're not too cold," he told Tadmore.

"You're very polite. Did she miss out on the politeness course?" She gestured toward Flemming.

"You're not still angry about her comments, are you?"

"She had no right to give me a hard time because I let Sara take a shower. She wasn't there. She didn't find Sara. She didn't see her like that. I couldn't think of anything else to do."

"You're right; she wasn't there." He said, "Flemming, go inside and help them finish up. I'd also like to see you in my office tomorrow."

"Yes, sir." She scurried toward the warmth of the house.

They got in the car. Niall started the engine and turned on the heat.

"It's very cold, but it shouldn't last too long. The weather people say it's going to snow soon. It always gets warmer when it snows."

"I don't feel like making small talk right now," she replied testily.

"You'll have to talk to me sometime."

"What do you want from me? All I did was find my best friend locked in a closet."

Niall gave up for the moment. She might be right. Maybe he didn't need anything from her. Why was he pushing her?

"Turn left at this corner," she said.

"Where do you live?"

"135 Maple Drive."

Niall was impressed by the neighborhood. It was an older part of town but still in good shape with plenty of tree-lined streets, small gardens, quiet, and with a good school. They'd looked at houses there before Maggie's illness. The familiar sense of loss began to rise in him.

Anne said, "You know, don't you?"

"About you and Martin? Yes."

"God, I'm such an idiot." She covered her face with her hands.

He pulled up in front of her house.

"I'd like you come to my office tomorrow." He handed her his card. "Call me and we'll set up a time."

She started to get out of the car, but Niall gently took her arm.

"I'm not convinced Martin is responsible for what happened to your friend. He may be in trouble himself, so anything you can tell us would help."

She looked at him skeptically, then pushed open the door and got out. She turned back. "What's that funny accent you have?"

"Accent? I don't have an accent." He smiled; many people had asked him that question. It had been the same in Ireland. He didn't have an Irish accent or a strictly American one, and at times he didn't know where he belonged.

She smiled before she closed the door. Niall waited until she had gone into the house and turned on the lights before he pulled away, echoes of her smile resonating inside him. For the first time in ages, he felt an emptiness that craved fulfillment. Anne of the good luck, with her green eyes, would require more of his attention; she reminded him of the spéirbhean, the fairy woman. Niall played with the impression on the drive to his empty house. What was it about her?

He lay in bed for hours, trying to drag the slippery impression to the surface. His thoughts eventually drifted to Maggie and then to his father. For the ten thousandth time he relived the night of his father's murder:

"Niall me boy, would you recite a poem for your old father before he sets off to work?" Niall O'Huiginn Senior had said to his son in Irish.

"I would certainly, but Da, why are you going to work tonight?" said the six-year-old Niall.

"I'm doing a reading at school. Come on now, give us a poem. You remember how granddad had one if a fly landed in his tea. And your uncle Ciarán has one for every pony in the fields. He always said a good poet is never without words. Come on now, it would make my heart sing for the rest of the night if you would."

Niall smiled.

His mother Noreen said, "Go on now, young Niall, give him his poem or he'll be late."

"All right, should I say it in Irish or in English?"

"Will you listen to him?" His father slapped his hands on his knees and smiled. "English would be fine and I haven't got all night; people are waiting for me."

Niall had begun writing an aisling – a dream or vision poem – in secret weeks earlier, but he hadn't been able to finish it. His father had taught him all the famous ones, including their structure: the 12th century poem, The Vision of Mac Con Glinne; the 16th century aislings of his ancestor, Tadhg Dall O'Huiginn; Egan O'Rathaille's 17th century poem, Brightness Most Bright; and even the 20th century Aisling by Austin Clarke.

The beautiful woman ran and the weary poet chased her, needing to discover her secret. In many of the poems, the woman represented Ireland. What were the subtleties of the aisling form that his father called the richest verse? His da understood the stressed meters, the lyrical nature, and the decorations he spoke of so often. It was the poet's loneliness that conjured the woman from the mist. The poet needed this muse, and the fulfillment the spéirbhean brought. The elusive beauty, giving and taking at the same time. Women.

Six-year-old Niall hadn't understood. Even now, he wasn't sure he understood the poetic form or women; some intangible part remained out of reach.

Doubt gripped him, but he decided his father would be pleased and surprised if he recited it, so he'd cleared his throat and began:

One cold winter morning,
before the birds began to sing
a troubled woman appeared to me.
The film of sleep clung to my eyes, and
my spirit fought to break the spell.

Trapped, I listened.
Hesitant, she began her tale
and the words dripped, slowly,
like cold honey from her ruby lips.
Her green eyes sparkled like bright flames.

Her milky form and fairy hair shone like the sun
shimmering off the oceans of Mac Lir,
her pale lily skin reflected the torment
of the thorn reaching for the rose petal,
and I believed all she said.

"That's all I've written. I don't know how to finish the poem."
"It's grand, son."
"But I haven't finished it, yet."
"Indeed, I heard you the first time, but it's a beginning. Now, tell me where in the name of God did you learn about women?"
"I don't know."

"I thought so. One of these days we'll have a talk about them, and then you'll be able to finish the poem, but I must be off now. We'll talk more about poetry and women when I return."

"All right, Da."

He winked at young Niall. Niall watched his father kiss his mother, and he was glad to see them kiss, then his father hugged him and said, "Take care of your mother until I come home, and be a good boy now."

Young Niall slipped one of his plastic soldiers into his father's pocket, knowing his father would find it and maybe smile again. "You know I will. I'll watch everything, just like I always do."

"Good enough." They were the last words Niall ever heard from his father.

He'd gone back to playing with his soldiers, disappointed that his father had to leave but happy he had liked the poem, and would help him finish the aisling.

An hour and a half later, the doorbell had rung. Niall had been lying in bed. People never came to their house when his father wasn't home, so Niall slipped from under the cover and hid behind his partially open bedroom door to see who was there. It was an unhappy-looking police officer named O'Hara, who said he had very bad news. Niall's father had been shot two blocks away. He was dead, his wallet and briefcase were gone. Random street crime, the officer said.

The words had echoed endlessly through his head for the last thirty years. Niall had delivered the same news, using the same words – random street crime – to a hundred relatives of victims and choked on them each time.

———

The three verses of his still-unfinished poem played over and over in his mind like a broken record, until he eventually fell asleep.

The phone was ringing; he answered it on the fifth ring.

"Sorry to bother you, Lieutenant, but we've got one for you," Mettler said.

"What time is it, and who's dead this morning?"

"It's a few minutes after five. We haven't identified him yet, but that's not the half of it. The body is at Ms. Collins' and Ms. Tadmore's house."

"I left Anne Tadmore there. Is she all right?"

"She flew the coop before the call came in. Mr. Sneider, their neighbor from across the street, told one of the officers that he saw her drive away. He thought it was unusual for her to leave so early. Our best estimate is that she left several minutes before we received an anonymous call saying that someone had been shot at the house."

* * *

CHAPTER IV

Niall turned onto Maple Drive. It had been only a little over seven hours since he'd dropped Anne Tadmore at that front door. Several units were already on the scene. He parked away from the commotion, slipped a cassette into the player, and settled back for a few moments to listen and watch the street.

The first notes of 'Red Haired Mary' reminded him of a cool fall night five years ago when he'd responded to a report that a young man had been stabbed to death. This same song was playing that evening and he stayed in the car because he wanted to hear the end of it before dealing with the death. He'd casually watched the crowd of onlookers and had noticed a distraught-looking young woman with blood on her jacket slipping into the back of the crowd. He got out of the car and eased over to stand next to her. Black mascara tears lined her face. Niall had driven away with her before the crowd knew what had happened. She'd offered no resistance. The quick results earned him a commendation and started a ritual. The chances of picking another suspect out of a crowd were extremely slim, but listening to music gave him a few minutes to collect his thoughts.

An older model green Honda drove up the street. Niall had noticed the car drive by when he first arrived and now it was here again, which aroused his curiosity. The car slowed and passed Anne's house. Niall moved to the passenger's side hoping to get a closer look, but it was still too dark to see much beyond that the driver was a man. The license plate light was broken, and the car was gone before he could open his door. Niall reluctantly shut off the engine and stepped out of the warmth and into the cold. He walked toward the small crowd, inspecting the street and fighting off the sub-zero winds.

"Good morning, Lieutenant," Mettler said.

"Morning. I see everything is under control."

"Yes, sir."

"An older model green Honda drove by twice while I was in the car, but I couldn't get the plate number or see who was in it. Tell everyone to keep their eyes open. It's probably nothing, but I'd like to know who is so interested that they'd drive down the block twice so early on a Saturday morning."

"Done, sir." Mettler jotted details in his notebook.

"Well, what have we got?"

"The deceased is in Ms. Tadmore's bedroom. One shot from a small-caliber pistol to the back of the head. It was probably a .25 caliber but we haven't found the weapon. It appears he was sitting in the chair when he got it. It's an Indian guy – you know from India."

"I'm still with you. Keep going."

"He had no ID on him. There's a broken window in the kitchen door that someone covered with a piece of cardboard. We found pieces of glass on top of the garbage and small pieces on the floor around the door. We also found scissors used to cut the cardboard and the tape still on the counter. We're assuming he or they entered through that door, possibly after Ms. Tadmore left, because the cardboard was dangling by one piece of tape. There are no signs of a struggle, but there are marks on the carpet that look like someone dragged the guy upstairs, put him in the chair, then shot him."

"Any word on the location of Miss Tadmore?"

"No, but we have an APB out for her and her car."

"What do you think? You met her. Do you think she did it?"

"You spent more time with her than I did, sir."

"I know but I'm asking your opinion."

Mettler lowered his notebook and stared into the darkness before he replied. "Why would she put someone in her bedroom and kill him? She's young and looks strong, but I doubt if she could drag the guy upstairs. Now, if it was Martin Charon who'd been shot, I might say yes, but at the moment, I don't see it, so I guess I'm saying I don't think she did it."

"O.K. Who made the call?"

"The dispatcher said a man called from the house, but surprise, surprise, he didn't give a name."

"Did he, by chance, have an accent?" Niall asked.

"There was no mention of an accent. The caller only said there was a body at this address. The first unit arrived within five minutes. The forensics technicians checked the phones: the ones downstairs had prints, but the phone in Ms. Tadmore's room was wiped clean, so he might have called from there. That's all we have right now. The ME's people are standing by to take the body, but I asked them to wait until you had a look before they move it."

"I might as well get it over with so they can finish."

The two-story wooden beam and stucco house was a New Jersey attempt to update a Tudor home but the attempt had failed. The dim light at the front door didn't offer a warm welcome. Niall pushed open the door remembering watching Anne Tadmore do the same thing. He entered the modestly furnished living room that gave a sense of hominess and warmth, in spite of the body waiting upstairs for his inspection. Two technicians taking pictures each nodded to Niall.

The first floor had a living room, dining room, kitchen, and a small study to his right. There were three windows in the living room, each covered with white sheers topped by blue drapes. Two oak end tables sandwiched a well-used but clean green velvet couch. The tables' matching cut-glass lamps cast rainbow sparkles on the walls. An old brown leather recliner sat next to the nearest table; it faced the television and the small fireplace. There was a matching oak dining room table with six chairs, which sat between the couch and the door to the kitchen. The walls displayed a collection of family photos. He recognized Anne in the pictures and the good-looking woman with long blond hair must be Sara Collins. Several photos of a young Anne who was with her parents or so Niall assumed, and then with Sara and a man he guessed to be Sara's father in many of the others. He continued his inspection and noticed a wet spot on the carpet near the kitchen door.

"What's this?" he asked a nearby technician.

"Someone spilled a drink."

Niall looked around the room. There was a brandy snifter and a book of matches on the table next to the couch. The area had already been dusted for prints so he picked up the glass, which had a small amount of liquid in it. Niall sniffed the aroma of apples and alcohol. He replaced the glass and picked up the book of matches, from Sammie's Restaurant and Bar. He had been there a few times, but Maggie had preferred elegant restaurants.

He scanned the room for the bottle, but didn't see one. He sat in the beat-up recliner next to the couch and tried to imagine Anne sitting here watching television with a drink in her hand – and then shooting a man in the back of the head. An explanation for the spilled drink eluded him. Had it been an accident? The room was neat and orderly, but nothing like Charon's house. Mettler was right: There were no signs of a struggle.

He went into the kitchen and searched all the cabinets, but there was no alcohol. The crime scene technicians had pulled the plastic garbage can from under the sink; it sat in the middle of the floor. The broken window shards were on top of the garbage, but he didn't see an empty liquor bottle. The piece of cardboard still dangled from where it had covered the broken pane.

He told the technician. "You can bag the garbage now, and put the cardboard back in place, would you? It's too cold to leave it like that."

Niall headed upstairs, stopping to look in the small study to the right of the front door. It looked like no one had been in it in a long time; it had a few chairs and a moderate amount of cobwebs swaying in the currents of circulating heat. The upstairs landing was relatively small. Three bedroom doors and the bathroom door stood open. Two workers from the ME's office told him all the rooms had already been processed.

Niall entered the bathroom. It was small, clean, and had the sweet smell of soap and shampoo from a recent shower; the clear plastic shower curtain still had a few drops of water on it. He counted fifteen different types of shampoo and ten different conditioners. "These women must love to shampoo their hair," he said to no one in particular. The medicine cabinet and under sink revealed nothing suspicious.

Sara Collins' bedroom was cluttered, but decidedly feminine. The room smelled of lavender, small bunches of dried roses hung on the light peach-colored walls and the comforter had a peach floral print. A silver-framed black and white photo of a young couple sat on her dressing table next to a purple address book.

Niall opened the book and flipped through the pages. Sara had written comments and had drawn flowered designs next to the names and numbers. One of them was surrounded with hearts: The name was Joe Madera, and the comment next to it was 'Anne's true love?' The words were written in different colored inks – Sara Collins had spent a good deal more time on this name than on the others. He stuck the book in his pocket.

The second bedroom appeared to be a combination guest room and office. A twin bed sat in one corner against the wall; a shiny white dresser was on the opposite wall; an old oak desk with a desktop computer sat in front of the window. The closet door was open revealing a black metal two-drawer filing cabinet tucked in the corner. Niall looked through both drawers, which contained files with customer names, receipts from Mel's House of Color and invoices. Two boxes of papers on the closet shelf overflowed with Sara and Anne's income tax papers going back several years. He moved to the last upstairs room. It was also feminine, but the colors were dark, gloomy maroons, and blue-grays. Anne must not like bright colors he thought.

The body still rested on a small chair by the dresser in the dimly lit room. A small trail of coagulating blood ran down the corpse's back and pooled at the base of the chair leg. The dead man's hands were folded in his lap. Not a hair on his head was out of place. Had the murderer combed it? It must have been done after he had been shot. Was the body staged and placed on the chair to be photographed?

He went to the window, pulled back the heavy curtains, and looked at the frosty world outside. The sun would be rising soon, but he didn't think the eerie quality would disappear from the room.

Mettler entered. "Lieutenant, the boys asked me to ask you if you're finished."

"Yes, I've seen all there is to see here."

Niall walked out of the room, and the ME's men lifted the body off the chair.

"Everyone's ready to leave unless you need them for anything."

"No Anthony, I'm sure they've done everything. Tell them I want reports as soon as possible. Did that car come by again?"

"I've been looking for it since you told me, but I haven't seen it. When I came inside, I left a man to keep watch. It may have been only a rubber-necker." Mettler massaged his close-cropped hair, a habit he had whenever he felt uncomfortable.

They walked back into the cold night air. "Is there a problem?" Niall asked.

"You've been acting a bit odd since last night, sir."

"Is that so? Don't worry about it. It's just a phase I'm going through."

"Good, because I thought maybe you were thinking of getting involved with Ms. Tadmore."

"Whatever gave you that idea?" Niall replied, curious if Anthony could be right.

"I saw the resemblance when I walked into the kitchen."

"What are you talking about?"

Mettler's face reddened. "I thought for sure you'd seen it, sir. She looks…that is, Ms. Tadmore bears a striking resemblance to Maggie."

"Really? Are you sure?"

"Pretty sure, sir."

Niall was puzzled and a bit concerned that he hadn't noticed the resemblance. He desperately wanted to go back in and take one of the photos of Anne so he could compare it with one of Maggie, but he fought the urge and instead he smiled at Mettler to allay his fears.

Mettler continued, "You know Joan is away visiting her family, in California."

Niall wondered what he was leading up to now.

"She wants me to…that is, we'd like to invite you to dinner when she comes back."

Niall stopped and pulled the collar of his overcoat tighter around his neck. He didn't want to alienate Mettler and wasn't sure how he felt about being set up by his wife again. All the signs were pointing for him to carry on with his life but he fought them. Although he had promised Maggie that he'd find another love, the thought of looking for someone to take her place was unappetizing.

"That's really kind of her. Let me know what she has in mind when she returns," he said. "In the meantime, I think we've done everything we can here. I'm going to the office. I found a phone book in Sara Collins' room and want to check some of the numbers. Find out everything you can about Charon and Anne. Then we'll talk to Sara Collins. She might be able to give us more information after a good night's sleep and some food. Let me know as soon as we get an ID on the body."

"Yes, sir."

"I'm sure Charon is up to his neck in this mess. While it's not him in there, it could be one of the men who came to visit him the other night. One last thing, Anthony: Have a unit cruise the neighborhood to see if they can find that green Honda."

* * *

CHAPTER V

Niall returned to his office hung up his coat and glanced at the icicle, which still clung stoically outside his window.

He sat at his desk and opened the address book. The paper was thick and heavy. He read each page carefully. On his third pass, he decided to call "Anne's True Love". He dialed Joe Madera's home number first. It rang four times before the answering machine picked-up. Madera's message said only "leave a message." Niall left his name and number then called Madera's work number.

"Royal Court Hotel, how may I help you?" a female voice said.

He was familiar with the showy hotel by route 9, but jotted its down name anyway. "I'd like to speak with Joe Madera, please."

"I'm sorry; he's not in right now. May I take a message?"

"It's rather important that I speak with him. Can you tell me what hours he works?"

"I'm sorry, sir, but I'm not authorized to give out that kind of information."

"Would you connect me with the person in charge then?"

"And who may I say is calling?"

"Lieutenant O'Huiginn of the Hilltop Police."

"Yes, sir, one moment please. I'll connect you with the manager."

Niall was left hanging for several minutes listening to soft music aimed at keeping him calm as he speculated about Joe Madera and Anne. Had he dumped her or had she dumped him on her quest for Martin Charon? Were they still friendly? He wasn't at home or at work. Could they be together?

Someone finally picked up at the other end of the line and a woman said, "Lieutenant O'Huiginn, I'm so dreadfully sorry for leaving you on the line so long, but I had an emergency. Although, I guess you know all about emergencies. In any case, I apologize. Now, you want to know about Joe Madera. Has he done something wrong? Is he in some kind of trouble?"

"No, no, he's not in trouble. I just need to speak with him about a matter I'm investigating. With whom am I speaking, please?"

"How rude of me, I'm the general manager, Gennifer Bidon. Gennifer with a G."

"Can you tell me when he works? I tried his home, but he's not there either."

"How odd, he usually goes straight home." She paused. "Joe works from ten at night until six in the morning Tuesday through Saturday."

"I suppose he'll be there this evening then?"

"He's always here. Joe has a perfect work record. He's such a good night manager. He usually arrives around nine-thirty PM."

"Thanks for your help, Mrs. Bidon. I'd like to leave my number in case you hear from him sooner."

"It's Miss Bidon, and I'm sure he'll be more than happy to assist you. I know him, and he's always willing to cooperate."

She continued to heap free-flowing superlatives on Madera until he hung up. Joe Madera must be a hell of an employee, he thought, or maybe Miss Gennifer Bidon with a G was more than a general manager to him.

Niall looked at the phone and then began the tedium of calling all the numbers in it. Some were no longer in use and a fair number didn't answer. He left messages asking them to call Mettler. None of the people who answered admitted to having seen Anne Tadmore or Sara Collins in months. He closed the book after the last person apologized for not being able to help and promised to call if they heard from Anne.

The patrol units in town and the departments from the county and surrounding towns had descriptions and photos of Anne Tadmore and Martin Charon. The forensic reports hadn't come in yet. All he could do for the moment was wait and see what happened next. He looked at the year-end statistics reports still piled on his desk and decided to finish them while he had the chance. He went to work.

Two hours later Mettler stuck his head into his office. "Excuse me, sir. I thought you'd want to know that I finished the paperwork from last night. I also received the lab report on Ms. Collins, and it's inconclusive if she was raped, but they did find traces of semen on the bed."

Niall dropped his pen on the desk and stretched. "She didn't say anything about having sex with Charon before the two Indian men arrived, did she?"

"No, sir, but she probably wouldn't, under the circumstances."

"We'll go and have a few words with her this afternoon."

"Meanwhile, I want to run something by you that's been bothering me."

Mettler said, "I'm all ears."

"I found this address book in Sara Collin's room. She has notes and little drawings next to almost all the numbers. However, one is on a page by itself and more highly decorated than the others; it has hearts and flowers surrounding it and a message that says "Anne's true love?" with a question mark after it. Why would Sara have spent so much time on this number, and what does that question mark mean?" He showed Mettler the page.

"My wife doodles when she's on the phone, sir. Maybe Sara Collins does too."

"She would have had to spend a lot of time talking to Joe Madera to do all this doodling. Could it be that she's in love with Joe Madera, too?"

"I don't know, sir. It sounds very complicated and incestuous. I'm going to lunch soon. Do you want a sandwich?"

"I would, thanks; make it tuna on a hard roll, if you don't mind." Niall handed him ten dollars.

He went back to work on the files. A half hour later, the phone rang.

"This is Joe Madera. Sorry I didn't call you sooner. I went to sleep after work, and I'm in the habit of turning off the phone." The voice was upbeat and confident.

"That's O.K. Thanks for calling. I wanted to speak with you about Sara Collins and Anne Tadmore. You know them, don't you?"

"For years."

"Have you heard what happened to Miss Collins last night and about the incident at their house early this morning?"

"I just heard about Sara and the murder on the noon news. When I listened to your message, I knew it had to be related. It's awful. Who would do that to poor Sara? She's so kind and lovable."

"That's what I'm trying to find out. Have you seen or heard from Anne Tadmore?"

"No, I'm sorry I haven't. As a matter of fact, it's been a few months since I spoke to either Sara or Anne. I wish Anne would call me."

"What about Martin Charon? Do you know him?"

"No. I've never met him. Anne told me all about him, though."

"Miss Tadmore and Mr. Charon are missing. If you have any ideas where either of them might be, it would be very helpful."

"I've been pretty busy with work. I have a new girlfriend, too," Madera added with a somewhat conspiratorial chuckle. "You know how it is with women. They don't like hearing about old girlfriends." When Niall abstained from joining in the male bonding, Madera continued. "Anyway, let me think for a second. Anne used to go to her parents' grave whenever she needed to work out a problem; they're buried at Calvary Cemetery. Although, I guess it's too cold for her to spend much time there right now. As for Charon... I don't know. Have you checked the university? He always had something going on over there with the Indian students or one of the coeds." Madera accentuated the last word.

"He's a real ladies' man then?"

"He's a dog, a big-time dog. He leaves his mark, and then moves on to the next one. He uses them."

Niall understood Madera's hostility. "What about Sammie's restaurant? Does that mean anything to you?"

"Sammie's! Hell, I used to go to dinner there sometimes with Anne, but it's not a place she'd go to hide."

"I'd appreciate a call if you think of anything that might help us locate either of them."

Niall hung up. The conversation left him wanting to talk face to face with Madera, but he didn't know exactly why. Something in his voice had made Niall uncomfortable. Madera had been too jovial and friendly. He said he'd never met Charon, but he knew a lot about his likes. He needed to look him in the eyes. Niall stretched and strolled to Mettler's desk.

"Joe Madera says he hasn't had contact with any of our trio for the last few months. He also says he has a new girlfriend, but he seemed a little too adamant about it. I thought it was curious that he didn't seem concerned about Anne Tadmore's disappearance. A look at Anne and Sara's phone records is in order."

"It's Saturday, sir. It'll take some time to get them."

"At the moment all we have is time, Anthony." He went back to his office.

The pile of folders grew smaller as the afternoon slipped away, and Niall still had no word about the missing duo. He had sent a patrol unit to check the cemetery, but there was no sign of Anne. The university police searched the campus, but didn't turn up the elusive Charon. At three o'clock, a patrol unit ticketing cars at expired parking meters found Anne Tadmore's locked white Mazda RX7. Niall sent a unit to keep an eye on it in case Anne, or someone else, came for it.

Niall put the last of the reports on the finished pile. His mind hadn't been on them too much toward the end, and he hoped he hadn't made any mistakes. He kept wondering about Anne. Was she on foot? Was she with Charon, or were they both lying dead somewhere? Was Madera telling him the truth? What had gone wrong, and had the murderer lugged the body up the stairs and into her room?

Niall opened his bottom desk drawer and looked at the eight by eleven framed photo of Maggie until he felt the sadness emerging. He closed the drawer, took a deep breath and let it out slowly. The winter sun would be setting soon, and he needed some action to change his mood. Time to see Sara Collins. She might be able to resolve some of his unanswered questions.

He grabbed his coat and walked into the hallway, where he ran into Flemming.

"I was just coming to see you, sir."

"Let's talk a minute."

Her jaw muscles tightened and her lips drew thin; a deep crease appeared between her eyebrows that hadn't been there last night. He didn't want to berate her too much for her run-in with Anne, but he had to say something. Arguing with Anne had been unprofessional. He'd heard other reports that Flemming's outspoken behavior verged on harassment of both victims and perps. She needed time to reflect before she landed in real trouble.

"Did you take the sensitivity course?" he asked.

"Yes, sir."

"Well, I don't want to hear another complaint or you'll be taking the course again."

"But sir, won't you even listen to my side of the story?" Her face grew redder and the crease deeper. She was ready to burst.

"Go ahead, but make your explanation quick."

"I was the first on the scene. Anne Tadmore was hostile and uncooperative from the moment I arrived. I called a supervisor and requested an ambulance and as soon as Sergeant Boehm arrived, I separated the two women. I took that woman into the kitchen and attempted to question her at Sergeant Boehm's request, but she grew more abusive. I was only trying to keep the situation in hand when you arrived."

Niall was glad he hadn't been the first on the scene. Flemming had probably taken the brunt of Anne's hostility by the time he arrived.

"Is that it?"

"Yes." She shuffled her feet.

"Tell Sergeant Boehm I have a job for you. I want you to go to the hospital and keep an eye on Sara Collins. Stay outside her room, and make sure she stays healthy. Do you understand?"

"Yes, sir."

"I'm on my way there now with Mettler. I'd like you to be at her door before we leave the hospital."

The crease between Flemming's eyes disappeared along with her fear of punishment. Niall watched her go and then went to find Mettler.

"Let's go, Anthony. Maybe we'll get there in time for one of those nice hospital dinners."

* * *

CHAPTER VI

Saint Mary's Hospital was years past its best days. Air pollution had mixed with snow, rainwater, pigeon droppings, and time to muddy its once-white facade.

Sara's doctor was on the third floor, talking to a nurse.

Niall stuck his badge between them and introduced himself.

"Yes, what can I do for you? I already told the Sergeant everything just a few hours ago."

"You said it didn't look like Sara Collins had been raped."

"There were no signs of tearing or bruising, and the lab didn't find any traces of semen. What more can I tell you?" The doctor didn't look at them but studied papers in his hand.

"How is she otherwise?"

"Emotionally, she appears to be doing very well, but I can't predict how she will deal with the psychological trauma in the long term; it isn't my area."

They left and headed downstairs to find room 204.

"Doctors," Niall mumbled.

They moved through subtle walls of ever-changing odors at almost every step. One moment he smelled medication. In the course of an exhalation, the smell became the acrid odor of sickness, and then that too was washed away by a wave of antiseptic chemicals. He hated the smells. They reminded him of his time here with Maggie. They reminded him of pain.

"What more did you think he'd tell you, sir?" Mettler asked as they approached the second floor.

"I don't know, but there's something bothering me."

"Really, sir. Who would ever have guessed?"

Niall smiled as he pushed open the door on the second-floor landing, then squinted because of the harsh fluorescent lighting. Flemming was standing outside a door down the hallway, looking very official.

"I guess we know where room 204 is."

"What's Deborah doing here?" Mettler asked.

"I told her to come because I don't want anything to happen to Sara Collins."

"There's no evidence that anyone would want to harm her any further."

"Maybe, but I have a bad feeling. I don't think it will go away until we find Charon and Anne."

As they approached Flemming, she snapped him a salute. "I checked on her a minute ago. She's doing well."

Niall knocked on the door, then opened it without waiting for a response. Sara Collins was sitting in bed. Madera had been right: she did look lovable with an air of delicacy and innocence about her. She could have been a teenager instead of a 28 year-old woman.

"Good afternoon, Miss Collins. I'm Lieutenant O'Huiginn, and I think you might remember Sergeant Mettler from last night. How are you feeling today?"

"A little out there. I'm not sure if it's the drugs or maybe disbelief. The doctor says I've been traumatized, and it will take some time for it to go away."

"I'd like to speak with you for a few minutes, if you feel up to it?"

"Sure, I'm tired of staring at the wall."

Niall moved closer to the bed while Mettler slipped around the other side and faded into the background. She looked frailer than in the photos he'd seen at her house. In most of them, she'd been smiling or outright laughing, and her hair looked in constant motion. Now, her long blond hair rested motionless on her shoulders and the pillow. A white bandage covered her forehead.

"Actually, I was getting a little depressed sitting here all alone," she said. "Have you spoken to Anne? I called the house, but she's not there. I need to speak with her so I can straighten things out between us."

It never occurred to Niall that she didn't have access to the news. He glanced at Mettler, who stepped to the window and slipped his notebook from his pocket.

"How long have you been awake?"

"I don't know, probably most of the day. They don't let you sleep much in here. Every time I start to relax, someone comes and wakes me up to make sure I'm O.K. It could drive you nuts. I wasn't very tired anyway. I caught up on my rest while I was in the closet." She smiled weakly.

Niall smiled back, but it was forced; he hated giving people bad news. He decided to ask her some questions before he told her about Anne and the dead man.

"You and Anne have been friends a long time, haven't you?"

"Best friends all our lives. I only hope we still can be friends."

"I know you'd probably like to block the last few days out of existence, but I need you to try and remember what Mr. Charon and the two men said while they were speaking English."

"I've been thinking about it since last night, but it all happened so fast. Martin went to the door, and I ran into the kitchen." Sara stopped talking and her pale skin reddened as she relived the events.

"Please continue. We're only trying to help."

"The whole situation was so frightening and embarrassing." She lowered her head.

"We understand. Just continue. It will help, believe me." She looked up and he smiled.

"I kind of remember the two Indian men were saying they didn't know about someone named Jim. Then one said something like, 'if they knew about Jim, they wouldn't have helped.' I'm sorry, but they were speaking very fast, and I was behind the door."

"You're doing great. What else did they say?"

"Martin said something in Hindi, and after that I didn't understand anything." She shrugged, which made her silky hair bounce on the pillow.

"That's very helpful. Did you sleep with Mr. Charon?"

Her face grew red again. "I'd remember if that happened. I mean, thank God it never got that far. I don't think Anne would ever forgive me if I had." She added, "When I was in the closet I kept thinking that God arranged the whole thing to prevent me from ruining our friendship."

Niall thought that might be carrying faith a bit too far, but who knew what God intended. He believed she hadn't slept with Charon but might have if they hadn't been interrupted.

"What is your relationship with Joe Madera?"

Sara smiled. "Joe is a friend. He was Anne's boyfriend before she met Martin. I used to talk to him a lot when Anne…how can I explain it?" She hesitated, mindlessly pulling at her hair while trying to find the correct words. "Anne became fixated on Martin about a year ago. We painted his house and sort of became friends. Anne fell for him very hard. She's never even been able to understand it herself. Anyway, that's when she started pulling away from Joe. They used to spend so much time together but within a month of meeting Martin, she hardly even spoke to Joe. Joe was devastated by her coldness; he called me several times a week to talk about her. Anne and I have separate lines."

"If Anne were in trouble, who would she ask for help?"

"What do you mean, trouble? Where's Anne? Oh God, has anything happened to her?" She threw the covers off and let her legs hang over the edge of the bed.

"Calm down." Niall took a step closer. "It won't help you or Anne if you get too excited. I'm sorry to have to tell you, but Anne is missing. She left the house this morning at about five-thirty, and hasn't been seen since. Who would she ask for help?"

"There's only one person besides me she'd ask for help: Joe." She'd said it without any hesitancy.

Niall glanced at Mettler.

"What was that look? There's something else, isn't there?"

"You've been very cooperative. I don't want to upset you any further, but I feel you're entitled to know the entire truth. We still haven't found Mr. Charon but have every hope of locating him soon. However, we did find a dead man at your house this morning."

Sara grabbed her stomach and sucked in a long breath of air.

Niall continued. "Your friend was seen driving off by your neighbor, Mr. Sneider, not long before we received an anonymous call about the body. We still haven't identified the dead man."

"Oh God!" Sara threw her hands over her face and began to cry.

Niall said, "Relax. It's not your fault."

Sara grabbed his hand. "You have to ask Joe. He'll know where Anne is. Please, go ask him."

"Take it easy, and don't worry. We'll ask him right now." Niall signaled Mettler, who left the room as quietly as he could. "If you remember anything else, there's a police officer right outside your door who can reach me anytime, anywhere. I'll let you know as soon as we find Anne."

Niall smiled at her as he gently pulled his hand away, even though he didn't feel like smiling. He was too angry with himself for not pushing Madera.

Mettler was talking with Flemming when Niall walked into the hall, and said, "Today is going to be the first day Mr. Madera misses work. I don't like it when people lie and waste our time."

"I'm with you, sir."

Keep a close eye on her." Niall said to Flemming hooking his thumb in the direction of the room.

"I'll stay right here until I'm relieved."

The sun was almost down and it was so cold, the air had no smell. Niall pulled his collar close and walked faster. Neither of them spoke until they were near the car.

Niall said, "At the moment we only have her word against his, but I tend to believe her. We could bring him in for questioning, but I don't want to rush off half-cocked. Madera works nights, so if Anne asked him for help early this morning, he would have been at the hotel. I'm going to talk to the hotel telephone operator to find out if a woman called Madera early this morning. He's probably still at home. Go to his house and wait outside. Take Herzog with you. See if it looks like he has company, and wait until I call. I doubt he'd hide her there, or at work, but you never know. If he leaves, follow him."

* * *

CHAPTER VII

The Royal Palms Hotel looked like it had been set down in the wrong place. The hue of pastel paints with bright fluorescent lights would have fit better in Hawaii or Miami. Pastel green palm fronds were painted on each of the sliding glass doors. Two live palm trees in the lobby were visible through the large glass entranceway; every time the doors slid apart, the cold air rushing in whipped the foliage. Niall had never before had any reason to come here, and on closer inspection of the place, he was glad.

He picked a spot near the door to park. Instantly, a bellhop ran out to meet him.

"Can I take your bags, sir?" the eager young man asked.

"I'm not checking in." He flashed his badge. "I'd like to see Gennifer Bidon. Is she still here?"

"Yes, sir, I saw her at the reception desk a few minutes ago. You can't miss her. She's the one with the big red hair."

The bellhop laughed, then ran ahead of Niall – either to get out of the cold or to avoid any more questions, but in either case, Niall had the impression that the woman was a joke to the employees. He followed the carpeted trail to his left and in a few seconds spotted the red hair.

At first, he thought she was sitting behind the check-in desk, but as he approached it, he realized she was standing. Gennifer Bidon's shocking mane of red hair pushed straight up from her scalp in an attempt to make her look taller than the five feet he guessed she was. She looked to be about 30 years old with a well-proportioned body, very fair skin and an attractive face.

"Excuse me. Are you the manager?" he asked.

"Yes, I'm Gennifer Bidon. How may I help you?" Her voice was crisp with a deep timbre that rang false.

"We spoke earlier today. I'm Lieutenant O'Huiginn."

"Has anything happened to Joe?" Her voice rose two octaves.

Niall knew she'd said it without thinking. The waiting guests and two employees stopped and turned toward her. He watched her face change back to its formerly professional expression as she realized how loudly she'd spoken, then she cast a disapproving glance at the pair behind the desk. Niall caught a quick exchange of a smile between the workers.

Gennifer Bidon became the hotel manager again. "Step into my office."

He followed her, a bit perplexed. Could Bidon be the new girl-friend Joe Madera made a point of mentioning? Niall couldn't help comparing the women. Anne was tall, and pretty. Gennifer Bidon was…well far from being Anne Tadmore. Yet Gennifer-with-a-G shared one quality with Anne: Both radiated an air of desperation.

Bidon led the few feet to her office and strode directly behind her raised desk. She dropped into a leather swivel chair and spun to face him.

"Sit down and tell me what I can do for you."

"I'd like to speak with the telephone operator who was on duty early this morning." Niall squeezed into an uncomfortably small chair in front of her desk, then found himself looking up at her. She had shadows under her eyes.

"Can you be a little more exact, time-wise?" Bidon asked struggling to maintain her professional façade.

"I believe the call would have come here between five-thirty and six-thirty."

"Then you'll need to speak with Gina, the operator, or Millie, the desk clerk. Unfortunately, neither of them is here at the moment. Perhaps, if you told me exactly what you were looking for, I could be of some help."

"I believe a woman called early this morning wanting to speak with Mr. Madera."

"I knew it." She spun her chair in a complete circle.

Niall watched her spin and wondered about her sanity. "You knew what?"

"I answered the phone this morning. I knew it was her, but he told me it wasn't." Her voice grew softer and more plaintive.

"Who?"

"That ex-girlfriend of his."

"You know about her."

She let out a short sarcastic laugh and snorted when she breathed in. The sounds irritated Niall.

"Are you usually here at that time of day?" he asked.

She studied him for a short minute, then spun her chair in another circle. When she faced him again she said, "Alright, I'm not ashamed to say it. I spent last night with Joe. Why shouldn't I? If it weren't for me, he wouldn't even be working here. He was a mess after that bitch dumped him. Did you know they were supposed to get married?"

"No, I didn't."

"Well they were, and I was left with a night manager who couldn't even do his work. I did it for him, though, and I took care of him, too. I did everything but wipe his butt. He walked around the hotel like a zombie for two months, crying and popping Xanax like candy. I spent every single night listening to his pitiful stories until I coaxed him back to normalcy. I deserved a bigger reward than I got from him last night."

Her face became red, clashing badly with her hair color. The room grew warmer with her passion. The employees laughed behind her back but didn't dare do it in front of her. She commanded fear and was probably a wild woman in bed, but he only found her frightening. He pitied Joe Madera and wouldn't want to be him when these two met again. It was clear that Madera had suffered much more after he lost Anne than he'd let on earlier in the day, and now he was going to suffer again.

"Please, relax and tell me what you remember." He felt like he'd said those same words a thousand times already that day.

She took a deep breath, ran a hand through her red mane and smoothed the front of her jacket.

"At five-forty this morning, I left the room we used last night. Joe stayed so we wouldn't be seen leaving together. That was my idea, but I guess from the reaction outside just now, that I was only fooling myself. I slipped out one of the back entrances, and then casually came in the main door. As soon as I reached the front desk, the phone rang. The clerk was busy with wake-up calls, and I was closer, so I answered it. A woman asked for Joe. I asked who was calling, and she said her name was Sara Collins. Her voice sounded weird, familiar, and I felt something was wrong, but I sent the call up to the room anyway."

Gennifer Bidon shook her head, barely able to contain her obvious frustration and anger. Niall was fascinated the way her facial expressions changed. The emotional roller-coaster ride of her love affair with Madera wasn't over.

"You didn't listen in on the conversation?"

"I would never do that, no matter how much I may have wanted to, but I was certain something wasn't right when Joe came down and told me he was sorry but he had to leave right away. We were supposed to eat breakfast together. He blew me off. The shit! After all, I did for him. He hears her voice and runs off."

"Thank you. That's all for now. I don't have to speak with the operators at the moment, but I'll send someone to take the desk clerk's statement. I hope things work out for you."

He stood, straightened his coat, and headed to the door.

"Will Joe be coming to work tonight?" her voice stopped him. She was ready to forgive him.

"I believe he'll be busy tonight," Niall said without turning. So much for a perfect attendance records and love on the job.

He sent word for Mettler to pick up Madera.

The drive to the office gave Niall the time to piece together the events of the last few days. Although, he didn't know exactly when this drama had started, his involvement began when Sara Collins lied to Anne about her trip to Washington, DC. Sara had surreptitiously made her way to Charon's house for a few days of unbridled fun. The doorbell had interrupted them; Sara had hustled into the kitchen in case Anne was making an unannounced visit, but it had been two Indian men who'd screamed at Martin about someone named Jim. Sara was knocked unconscious when one of them pushed the kitchen door open, and the next thing she knew, she was tied up naked in a closet. She stayed there for two days until Anne came looking for Charon. Anne found Sara and had her take a shower, which may or may not have washed away valuable evidence. Sara went to the hospital and Anne went home to do her own recuperating.

Anne was a story all on her own. Was she really supposed to meet Charon or was she out of control, like Gennifer Bidon?

Anne had taken a shower after Niall dropped her off at her house, then went downstairs for a drink. At some point, someone had broken into the house. If there was a struggle, it wasn't a serious one because nothing looked disturbed – unless, of course, if Charon had been the murderer; he might have cleaned up after himself.

Then, apparently, Anne decided to leave early on a cold morning. What had driven her from the house? The neighbor said she was alone. She must have had time to dress. He thought of her green parka. That would mean leaving had been her choice. Was she involved? She'd called Joe Madera to ask for help; obviously, he said yes and left Gennifer in the dust. Madera had brought her somewhere other than his house. He might or might not have gone to his own home to sleep after he'd left her. Madera probably needed some sleep after Bidon had finished with him. She was insecure about herself, her job, and her looks and probably worked out those sexual frustrations on Joe. Niall felt that he could rule Joe Madera out as the murderer. Could Gennifer have been lying too? Niall decided she wasn't that good an actor.

He parked and hurried into the warmth of City Hall and his basement office. He didn't mind the underground office. It was warm in the winter and cool in the summer. However, the city was growing and so was the department. In the spring, a new building would be built, and by the end of the summer, he'd have an aboveground office.

Mettler appeared in his doorway.

"Anthony, I didn't expect you here so soon. How'd it go?"

"No problem, sir. Mr. Madera looked like he was expecting us, and didn't make a noise."

"His boss must have called him. I should have known she would. Oh well, what did you tell him?"

"That he was under arrest for obstruction of justice and possibly as an accessory to murder."

"How did he take it?"

"Calmly. Probably too calmly."

"And there was no sign of Anne Tadmore?" Niall glanced to see if the stalactite was still outside. It was.

"No sir, we checked his apartment. He was alone. It didn't look like anyone had been there but him."

"Take him to the interview room. I'll be there in five minutes."

"Already done, sir," Mettler said as he left.

Niall waited a few minutes and found himself staring at the icicle again. It was exactly twenty-four hours since Mettler had first told him about the woman in the closet. His desk was finally clear of the reports, but one man was dead, two people were missing, a woman was in the hospital, and he was about to question a liar.

Mettler was waiting outside the interview room when he turned the corner.

"How's he doing now?" Niall asked.

"He's cooler than the weather outside, sir."

They entered the room. Joe Madera was good-looking with thick, wavy, brown hair and large brown eyes – in fact, he looked surprisingly like Martin Charon. Niall smiled and sat opposite him. Mettler took a seat in the corner, and pulled out his notebook.

"Good evening, Mr. Madera. We spoke earlier. I'm Lieutenant O'Huiginn, and you know the Sergeant."

"I remember him."

"You know why you're here, don't you?"

"I sure do. You spoke to Gennifer."

"Then there's no reason for us to bother with formalities. Where's Miss Tadmore?"

"Lieutenant, I'm sorry I didn't tell you, but I had two good reasons. The first was that Anne really needed to sleep, and the second was that I didn't want to get an old friend in trouble. I called in a favor, so Maxwell let her stay at his place."

"That's very noble of you, but do you realize you might have put both of them at risk?"

Madera stared at him, but Niall couldn't read his face.

"When Anne asked for my help I didn't know anyone had been murdered. Of course, I realized what had happened after I heard the news, but I want you to know that I've been in touch with Maxwell hourly since we spoke this afternoon. In fact, I called him right before the Sergeant dragged me out of my house, and Maxwell said everything was quiet, and Anne was still asleep."

Niall thought Madera's attitude was too friendly. It had a forced quality.

"Did you call your friend after Miss Bidon called you, or before?"

Madera squinted at him. "I know what you're thinking, but I'm not lying. Anne's still there. She's not running from you. She just wanted a place to sleep without being disturbed. I'm willing to bet she doesn't even know about the murder." He'd said it all rapid fire.

Niall refused to be Madera's buddy. "You didn't answer my question."

"I called after Gennifer called me. Maxwell's expecting you."

Madera gave them the address of a studio in an old warehouse area on the east side of town. His friend's name was Maxwell Good.

Niall pushed his chair away from the table and stood. "It would have saved us all so much trouble if you'd told me the truth this afternoon."

Mettler continued to write in his book.

"I'm sorry I didn't, but I feel better now that I've told you. Can I leave? I start work in a half hour."

Niall still didn't like Madera's overly friendly manner.

"You'll have to stay here until your information can be verified. We're not playing games. You're under arrest for obstruction of justice," Niall said before leaving the room with Mettler.

"Put him in a holding cell until the morning, Anthony. I'm going to check out Maxwell Good's place and see if Anne Tadmore is indeed there. I'll call and let you know." Niall began to walk away.

"If I'm not mistaken, Maxwell Good is one of our more famous residents, sir."

Niall stopped. Mimicking his uncle Ciarán, he said, "You are a font of knowledge. Then Mr. Good shouldn't be any trouble. What else can you tell me about him?"

Mettler grinned. "He reproduces old masterpieces and is well-known for his almost-perfect copies. Rich people pay big money for his work."

"I guess I better not keep him waiting. Stay here until I call and then go home to rest. I think we'll have another busy day tomorrow."

"Aren't you going to bring Miss Tadmore back here, sir?"

"That remains to be seen. If she is asleep, I'll leave her there until the morning. It's getting late, and I don't relish staying here all night. Do you?"

"I don't mind. My wife's away until next week."

"If the situation looks controllable, I'll send the unit watching her car to Maxwell Good's to keep an eye on them. In either case, I'll let you know."

Niall had been in the office only a half-hour, but the extreme cold had cooled not only the interior of the car but the engine as well. The temperature readout on the bank across the street said minus five degrees and he figured the wind chill probably brought the actual temperature down to fifteen or twenty below zero.

His drive across town was traffic-free and ten minutes later the old factory area came into view. He made a final right turn onto Monet Way where all the structures had been converted into artists' studios a dozen years earlier. The complex was maze like, but Niall had been out here on several occasions and had a general idea of the layout. The area wasn't well lit either and he made a wrong turn onto a dead-end street named Van Gogh Way. It took him two more turns onto streets named after other dead artists before he found Durer Way.

The addresses were painted in large numbers on the buildings. A single halogen light glowing outside Maxwell Good's address told him he was expected. The straight high walls funneled the bone-chilling wind.

He scurried to the metal door and knocked. A security camera covered with darkened plastic hung on the wall, its lens pointed at him. Niall wondered if Maxwell Good was watching him; he knocked a second time.

A cheerful voice from the intercom on his right asked who he was.

"Lieutenant O'Huiginn, Hilltop Police Department. Is that you, Mr. Good?"

"Come in out of the cold, Lieutenant."

The electronic door lock clicked. The interior was large with ceilings about thirty feet high, white walls and bright lights. The air smelled of paint and thinner. The exterior wall on his left was made of cinderblocks and opaque glass panels that started halfway up from the ground and ended a few feet from the roof. Two large gas heaters in the center of the ceiling blew warm air. The heat felt good.

The interior was broken into five sections. A kitchen with two doors was at the far end. On Niall's right was a workshop space with rolls of canvas, stacks of wood, saws, and paint-related materials. Further down he saw a large platform raised off the cement floor at the same level where the glass windows began. Japanese-style rice paper screens surrounded it. A narrow ladder to a hole in the platform floor was the only visible means of access.

On his near left was a combination office/relaxation area with a purple, glass-topped desk, a purple couch, some comfortable-looking purple chairs, and an entertainment center. Finally, further down on his left, was a circle of canvases with all the easels faced toward the center. The lower half of a man sitting on a chair with wheels was visible in their midst.

"Don't be bashful, Lieutenant. I'm down at this end."

Niall walked toward Maxwell Good, looking for but seeing no signs of Anne. The smell of paint grew stronger as he approached the canvases.

The famous artist wore a white lab coat streaked with paint, white sneakers, and baggy white coveralls. Maxwell Good had long purple hair and a white beard. Wire-rimmed glasses rested on the bridge of his nose. His face was thin, winter pale, and Niall guessed him to be in his late sixties. Three TV monitors sat on a table at the far side of his canvas circle, displaying the front door and two other outside views. One was in front of a large garage door; the other at the building's dark backside.

"This is quite the place you have here, Mr. Good," Niall said.

"It's quiet, Lieutenant. What part of Ireland are you from?"

"I was born in the west, but I've lived here most of my life."

"I was out in Roundstone a few years ago. It's a beautiful place," Good said without ever stopping his painting. His movements looked precise.

"I know it well."

Niall studied the canvases, all in different stages of completion. Some of them were vaguely familiar, but he couldn't pinpoint the artists or the periods. Art remained a gaping hole in Niall's education.

"See anything you like? I'll give you a discount." Good continued his brush strokes.

"I don't think I could afford one even with the discount. Is Anne Tadmore still here?"

"She's up there sleeping." Maxwell Good motioned with a paintbrush to the loft. "I've never seen anyone sleep as long or as soundly as her. She hasn't budged since early this morning, thirteen hours now."

Niall turned his attention to the loft. "If you don't mind, I'd like to see for myself."

"Be my guest." He dismissed Niall with a wave of his brush.

Niall climbed the ladder to the hole that served as the entrance to the platform and cautiously stuck his head through the opening. The floor was covered with carpet that matched the color of Good's hair and furniture. There was a large bed to the right and an oak dresser in front of him. The light was dim because of the rice paper screens surrounding the area, but he saw the outline of a human form under the covers of the large bed. Niall stepped closer. It had been over a year since he'd been this close to a woman in bed. His heart raced at the sight of her bare shoulder above the blankets and the sound of her soft breathing. He listened for a moment. Her breathing reminded him of Maggie and he tried to see if Anne really resembled her; he felt a little like a pervert but he had to know. He bent closer and studied her face in the dim light. What had Maggie looked like? He struggled to pull images from memory, but he'd spent all his time trying to bury them along with the pain. He closed his eyes to help remember. When he had her face in his mind, he opened them, and laid that image over Anne's face. They did look alike, the same tilt of eyes, the shape of her nose, the soft fullness of her lips and even the pixie-like ears. How could he have not seen the resemblance? His chest tightened.

Niall took a deep breath, moved away from her, and studied the area. Anne's clothes were neatly folded on the dresser, her bulky green parka thrown on a chair. He went back down the ladder.

"How well do you know Joe Madera?" he asked Maxwell Good.

"He saved my life. That's all I need to know about him."

The news shocked him. "How did that come about?"

"It was right after I received my first large check. My paintings had finally started selling. I was feeling damn good about myself and decided to do something wild to celebrate my looming success, so I went river rafting. Have you ever been river rafting?" He didn't wait for an answer. "By chance or fate, Joe and I were on the same rafting trip down the Colorado River. The water swirled around us. It was unnerving but exciting. Then we hit a rock, I felt a hand on my back, and I was out of the raft. I'd forgotten to close the buckles on my lifejacket and the raging water not only sucked me under but it also pulled the jacket right off me. Lucky for me, Joe jumped in and grabbed hold. We rode the rapids, breathing when we could and trying not to drink too much water. Then we hit a placid section and it was over."

Good never broke the rhythmic flow of his brushes until the end of the story when he turned to Niall and pointed the wooden end of a long thin brush at him.

"It was a hell of an experience and if it weren't for Joe, I wouldn't be here today. The most amazing part of the episode is that two months later I received a bill for the lost lifejacket," Good laughed.

Niall was surprised by the revelation about Joe Madera. Bravery wasn't a quality Madera exuded. Could someone have pushed Maxwell Good from the raft? Had it been Madera?

"Did you find out who pushed you out of the raft?"

Good stopped his whirling Dervish like painting and looked at Niall.

"I've thought about it a lot but never could remember who was sitting where. The raft jumped and bumped so much it could have been anyone. Maybe I just imagined feeling a hand on my back." Good stopped painting, but left his brush in place on the canvas as he looked at Niall over the top of his glasses. "You're not suggesting it was Joe who pushed me, are you?"

"No, not at all; it was a very brave thing he did. I'm not sure I would have had the courage to throw myself into a raging river."

However, Niall didn't like coincidences or unsolved mysteries and he didn't particularly like Madera.

"I don't think I would either, Lieutenant. I felt deeply indebted to him and would have given him anything in my power, but Joe hasn't asked for anything over the last seven years, so I sure was surprised when he telephoned this morning and told me he was calling in the debt."

Niall said, "That's about it for tonight. I'm not going to disturb Miss Tadmore, but I'm going to leave a car outside to make sure neither of you are disturbed. When she wakes, tell her I want to speak with her."

"Do you think she's in danger?"

"I can't be certain, but I'd like you to be careful. Don't let anyone in you don't trust or don't know. You seem to have an adequate security system in place."

Niall walked to the exit. He could still visualize the curve of Anne's exposed shoulder and hear the sound of her breathing. Had Maggie really breathed that way too? He struggled to remember as he opened the door, then stepped back into the howling night.

The car was cold again. He started the engine and called Mettler. He told him to send a car to watch the place, then asked about Charon, but there had still been no sign of him. After he hung up, he slipped a cassette of Irish harp music into the player and raced the engine to help warm the car.

Maxwell Good was a colorful and interesting man and apparently was also honorable. He tried to imagine jumping into a roaring, white-capped, mud-browned river to pull someone to safety but the memory of Anne kept reappearing in his mind's eye. Her shoulder looked soft and her breathing stirred something in him. Niall felt a surge of inspiration. He removed his notebook and a pencil from his inside jacket pocket, and scribbled words on the lined paper:

Torn by love and confusion,
lost in a world too lost,
she sought peace and happiness,
but death hunted this
daughter of Tír na Nóg.

Niall stared uncomprehendingly at the words for a minute and then as the warmth of the heater filled the car he realized that for the first time in thirty years he had written a new stanza of his unfinished aisling poem. The impression of warmth built in the pit of his stomach, spread through him and burst inside his head. He liked the sensation. The hunger he'd felt after dropping Anne at her house gnawed at him. Niall craved something: he craved life. His father's words popped into his head: "Indeed, I heard you the first time, but it's a beginning. Now tell me, where in the name of God did you learn about women?"

"I don't know," he'd answered shyly.

"I thought so. One of these days, we'll have a talk about them, and then you'll be able to finish the poem, but I must be off now. We'll talk more about poetry and women when I return."

But his da had never returned, and they'd never had that talk about poetry or women. The most important woman in his life had been Maggie. They were as close as he thought it possible for two people to be. She knew his every thought and mood, and he knew hers. He'd stayed with her throughout her illness, but hadn't dated other women since her death, even though she'd extracted a promise from him not to mourn. "Live for me. Live for us," she'd said. Now he wasn't sure he understood women the way his father had. Women had fawned over his father all the time, which had created tension whenever his mother questioned his father about other women, he say, "Stop your blather woman, you know you're the only one in the world for me."

His mother would laugh. "Listen to the original blatherskite himself. I'm no fool, Niall O."

What advice would his father have given him if he hadn't been murdered? Had he been waiting all his life for advice that would never come? He felt a hole in his knowledge. Maybe that was what had blocked the poem. He was waiting for that hole to be filled. He wasn't living.

Niall turned to a clean page in his notebook. The original stanzas were as fresh in his mind as if he'd just written them that very minute. He carefully printed them on the clean sheet of paper and added the new one at the bottom. He read them several times. The new one fit. Anne would help him finish the poem and maybe help him find something that had been missing from his life.

* * *

CHAPTER VIII

Sunday morning dawned icy clear, the sky the bluest Niall could remember having seen in years. Sara Collins was still hospitalized, he still had an unsolved murder and a missing Martin Charon, but he felt great. He'd located Anne Tadmore last night, and after almost thirty years, he'd found the inspiration to write more of the poem that haunted him.

As he entered, he checked to see if the icicle was still hanging outside his office window; it was. He turned to inspect the morning reports stacked neatly on his desk, along with the Fuji apple and the bottle of water Mettler always brought him. Mettler appeared as he took a bite from the crisp apple.

"How's our guest this morning, Anthony? Did he sleep?"

"He seems to have slept without too much difficulty, sir, and looks better than he did last night. What are we going to do with him?"

"I don't think he's done much harm, and we can't hold him too much longer without charging him, but I'd like to speak with him first. We'll turn him loose as soon as Anne calls."

"Anne, sir?"

"Don't say it. I'm not letting her get to me. I can't explain right now, but I'm fine."

"I hope so, but if you don't mind me saying, you seem strangely happy this morning. I haven't seen a look like that since Herzog got lucky with the cocktail waitress after the Christmas party."

Mettler took out his notebook and leafed through the pages. Niall waved the half-eaten apple at him to get his attention.

"Is the unit still sitting outside Good's place?"

"Yes, sir," he replied as he continued searching his notebook.

"Tell them to follow her when she leaves."

"Wouldn't it be easier for them just to pick her up and drive her here, sir?"

"You're right, as usual. Let's see what happens when she calls."

Mettler found what he was looking for. "We just learned the identity of the dead man, sir. His name is Satchang Ramdas, but he also goes by Jimmy Ramdas. He's only been in the country a few weeks. He gave his occupation as a private investigator."

"That's amazing. I never imagined that they might have PIs in India," Niall said.

"I never thought about it either but I don't see why they wouldn't."

Niall played with the pieces of data for a second. "Two Indian men at Charon's house and a dead Indian investigator found at Anne and Sara's house. Who or what was he investigating? Do you think he could be the 'Jim' the Indian men were talking about?"

"I'm sure we'll find out soon enough, sir."

"Did you get an address for him?"

"Ramdas entered the country as a tourist and gave a Manhattan hotel as his address. He had plenty of cash to back up his story and his papers were in good shape."

"One more thing before you go, Anthony: How do you always beat me to the office? No matter what time I arrive, you're already here."

"Kismet, sir, just kismet." Mettler left.

Niall began the daily chore of reviewing reports. After each file, he glanced at the clock; time moved slowly.

Eventually, the phone rang.

"O'Huiggin," he said.

"It's Anne Tadmore. I didn't kill that man. There was no one in the house when I left – and why did you arrest Joe? All he did was find me a place to sleep."

"Relax, you're not a suspect," he lied, "but we need to speak with you. And don't worry; I'm releasing Mr. Madera. Where are you?"

"I'm still at Maxwell's studio. He said he'd loan me a car. I'll be there as soon as I can. I just need to clean up a little."

Niall wondered if he should just tell her to go outside and get a ride from the detectives, but he needed her cooperation.

"Don't make any detours, Anne."

Niall called Mettler, and told him what had happened. He also told him to inform the detectives to follow Anne to the station and then to bring Madera to his office. Fifteen minutes later, they arrived, with Madera looking refreshed, but wrinkled.

"Jail seems to agree with you, Mr. Madera."

"I needed the rest, but I wouldn't want to make a habit of it."

He smiled, but Niall sensed tension behind his grin. His face was stretched too tightly. It might have been due to his night in jail, but something told Niall it wasn't that. It was, however, the first time Madera had missed work, and he was going to have to face the wrath of Gennifer Bidon; that, alone, was enough to make anyone anxious.

Niall told Madera, "I hope you will inform us if any facts pertinent to this case come to your attention. If I find you withheld more information, I'll go to the District Attorney. Do you understand?"

"You're the first person I'll call, Lieutenant."

"Good, I'm glad we understand each other. You're free to go now, Mr. Madera."

"Thanks, Lieutenant. I'm sorry for the trouble I caused." He left with Mettler.

Another hour passed, but Anne still hadn't arrived. After another 20 minutes, he called the detectives following her.

"She stopped to eat," Detective Herzog explained.

"Keep a close eye on her, and if she decides to make any more detours stop her and bring her directly to my office."

Forty-five minutes later Herzog called to say she was on her way and would be there in ten minutes. It was nearly noon, so Niall decided to go to lunch. There weren't many places open downtown on a Sunday afternoon, but he was hungry. He told Mettler to keep Anne there until he returned.

Niall stepped outside, but once in the bright sunlight he decided to wait for her. He leaned against the building, positioning himself to absorb the winter sun. He stood like that for several minutes, every so often turning his head to look for her. His feet were really getting cold and he was about to go when he recognized the bulky green parka walking toward him.

"Hello Lieutenant, are you enjoying the sunshine?"

"Yes, and I'm glad to see you arrived safely. Did you enjoy your breakfast?"

She looked behind her where Herzog was just getting out of the car.

"You had me followed?"

"We've been watching the building since last night, but it was for your and Mr. Good's protection. We wanted to make sure you were both safe."

"Maxwell told me you came by last night. He also said you came up and checked on me. I hope I wasn't talking in my sleep. I do that sometimes."

"You didn't make a sound. Shall we go inside?" Niall, fearing he might be acting too school-boyish, took a deep breath and settled himself.

"Yes, I'd like to get this over with."

"Don't worry. We don't use torture anymore."

"I'm not in trouble, am I? I didn't kill that man," she said.

"Don't worry," he repeated. "I'm hoping that with your help we'll be able to get a complete story of what happened at your house."

They passed through metal detectors, then a bored officer handed Anne a visitor's badge. There weren't many people in the corridors or on the elevator, and the sunlight dimmed the farther they went inside. Niall remained quiet, watching and learning what he could from her.

When they reached his office, Niall suppressed his excitement. He pulled a chair in front of his desk for her and went around the other side.

She said, "This looks like lead-based paint. You shouldn't be working in such an enclosed space. It's not good for your health." She switched topics without slowing. "I know you've been looking for me, but why did you put Joe in jail? He didn't do anything wrong."

"He's not in trouble at the moment. I brought him in because he lied to us."

"But I read in the paper that he was in jail."

"You shouldn't believe everything you read in the paper. While you've been sleeping, we've been trying to find out what happened at your house and at Martin Charon's. Unfortunately, we haven't had much luck."

"If Joe's not in jail, where is he?"

She apparently wasn't going to cooperate until she was ready. "He's probably gone home or to work. Any other questions?"

"How's Sara?"

"She's fine. I spoke with her yesterday. And your close friend, Officer Flemming, is watching her." He smiled, trying to break the tension.

"Very funny. I'm glad she's safe. And I'm relieved that my stupidity wasn't plastered all over the newspapers."

"Why did you run away? We were worried you might end up like Satchang Ramdas AKA Jimmy Ramdas," he said to test her reaction.

"Who?"

Her reaction was one of genuine puzzlement.

"The man we found dead in your bedroom."

"I can't believe someone was murdered in my bedroom. The last few days have been a nightmare. How am I going to sleep in that room again?"

"I don't know. However, now that you've had a long, long sleep and a good meal, you can tell me everything that happened, starting with Friday night."

Anne looked at the floor and said shyly, "Maxwell told me you're Irish. I knew you had an accent." She sat on the edge of the chair with her hands on her knees.

Niall smiled. "You're not flirting in an effort to draw my attention away from the business at hand, are you?"

"Oh, no, I'm not…It's just that…I'm really grateful you let me sleep. You could have pulled me out of bed in the middle of the night and dragged me down here."

The way she said it, and the memory of her exposed shoulder, gave her statement sexual undertones; Niall felt his face grow warm.

"But you didn't and I'm grateful for that." She smiled again.

"Anne, if we're going to resolve this matter, I need to know what happened Friday night and Saturday morning," Niall picked up a rubber band and twirled it around his index finger.

"I suppose you're right. It's gone beyond my obscene fascination for Martin. I can't even blame Sara for doing what she did. If it was me, I probably would have done the same."

"Good, I'm going to ask the Sergeant to come in and take notes."

Niall dialed Mettler's extension and in a minute, he entered the office, notebook in hand, and sat in the corner as unobtrusively as his size would permit.

"We're all ready. Begin with Friday," Niall told Anne.

"I made a date with Martin for dinner Friday night. I thought I'd try one last time to charm him." Her face flushed. "But when I didn't hear from him all week, I called Friday morning; there was no answer." She became more agitated. "I called several times that day but left only two messages. Around six, I started to wonder if he was sick or if maybe something was seriously wrong because he's a stickler about such things. He always says the most important things in life are to keep your word and to be prompt."

Her right hand moved hypnotically back and forth as she talked. She didn't appear to be conscious of the movement, but Niall realized she was avoiding eye contact.

"About seven-thirty I decided to walk over to check his house. The place was dark, but I used the extra key to open the back door. I didn't see anything, but did hear a scratching sound. At first I thought it was the cat, and then I saw Harry on the couch."

Niall remembered the cat snuggled on the living room couch amidst the people and activity around it. Anne grew more intense the more she described Friday's events. She sat so close to the edge of the chair he thought she'd fall off.

"I almost didn't go into the bedroom, but I forced myself to open the door and turn on the light. The room was a mess, and smelled like a gas station toilet. The scratching got more intense and I could tell it was coming from the closet. I picked up a heavy bottle of Martin's cologne for protection, opened the closet door, and there was Sara. I couldn't believe she was there. Strange, but the first thing that came to my mind was that she had lied to me. The closest person to me in the world had lied and Martin had lied too." She stopped, and shook her head. The memories were still too fresh.

"What did you do then, Anne?" he asked to keep her from dwelling on them.

"I helped Sara out of the closet and untied her. I pushed aside my surprise and anger, but I couldn't suppress them completely. You know what I mean?" She finally looked directly at him.

He knew she was referring to calling Sara a bitch.

"Then you helped her into the shower and called the police?"

"Yes. The rest of the evening went by in a blur. I remember Flemming talking to you and then you driving me home. I'm sorry I was uncooperative."

"Did you see or hear anything else before we arrived?"

"I don't think so."

"What happened after I dropped you at your house?"

"The first thing I did was take a shower. Then I sat down to have a drink of..."

"Calvados," said Mettler. The sound of his voice broke the connection between Anne and Niall.

Niall cast a harsh glance at him. "I believe Miss Tadmore is capable of telling her story without your help."

"Sorry sir, it slipped out."

"Continue, Anne."

"You know I drank Calvados?"

"You left the glass on the table, so it was no mystery. Please continue. We won't interrupt until you've finished. Isn't that right, Sergeant?"

"Exactly, sir." Mettler didn't look up from his notebook.

"I had the glass of Calvados to calm me down. Then I poured a second glass, sipped a little of it, and fell asleep. Sometime later I woke to the sound of breaking glass and heard noises coming from the kitchen. I was afraid it might be the same people who... who hurt Sara." Anne grabbed the arms of the chair. "I didn't know what to do. I had no time to call the police. I took my bottle of Calvados and hid behind the door between the kitchen and the living room. When someone stuck their head in, Wham, I hit him with the bottle and down he went. It was Martin."

Niall dropped the rubber band on his desk.

"At first I was afraid that I'd killed him but he was only unconscious. I threw the glass of Calvados in his face and he woke up. He sat on the couch, and I sat on my father's old recliner. I was going to call you and even had the phone in my hand, but Martin began telling me about a guy he met in India named Billy Ananda, who convinced Martin to smuggle jewels into the States. He hid the gems in a shipment of tea, he imports from Darjeeling. Martin is fanatical about chai."

"What's that?"

"It's a tea drink, sir," Mettler said.

"Thank you, Sergeant. I didn't know you held such knowledge."

"Glad to be of help, sir."

"Sorry for the interruption, Anne. Please continue."

"Did I tell you Martin loves tea?"

"You did."

"He told me that after the gems were successfully smuggled into the States…"

A light went on in Niall's head. Sara had said the men were talking about Jim, but she easily could have misunderstood. She was in the kitchen behind a closed door, and the men undoubtedly had Indian accents. They'd said gems – not Jim.

"Martin thought that would be the end of his dealings with Billy, but Ananda's friends started pushing him. They called, wrote letters, and even visited his classes, but Martin said he wouldn't do it again. Then Billy threatened to expose his smuggling activities to the university and the Indian government. Martin told me he gave in and helped them to save his job, his future, and the growth of his tea business. When the phone rang, Martin was afraid Billy's goons were calling. He was partially right. It was an Indian guy named Dr. Prabum something or other, who told me he was concerned about Sara's and my safety; he said to be careful until he arrived in town, and that he would explain everything that day. Martin acted weird throughout the entire phone call. I tried to ignore him, but it was really hard. By the way, Dr. what's-his-name called again. He must have left a message last night or this morning. I checked from Maxwell's car phone while I was driving here. He's in town and staying at the Long Arms Motel. He said he intends to visit Sara at the hospital for a little chat. Do you have any water?"

She'd spit out the entire story without stopping for a breath. Niall liked this Anne Tadmore better than the one he'd met the other night.

Mettler was at the door in one-step. "Would you care for anything, sir?" He left without waiting for an answer.

Niall swiveled his chair and checked the ice hanging from the window. Charon was smuggling gems. Could the Indian men have kidnapped him? Was Sara's condition some kind of retaliation because Charon hadn't done their bidding?

"Did you know that I'm the illegitimate daughter of Fatty Arbuckle?" Anne asked.

"I'm not ignoring you. I'm thinking."

"Actually, I'm used to being ignored by men."

He pivoted to face her. "I find it hard to believe that either you or Sara would have a hard time with men."

They looked into each other's eyes for a few seconds. She smiled shyly.

"Are you flirting with me, Lieutenant?"

Her question flustered him. "Just stating the obvious," he said. "What about Joe Madera? He seems to still like you."

Anne grimaced. "Joe is a good friend. He wanted to get married, but I didn't feel that way about him."

"I had the impression from both him and Sara that you were a couple until you met Charon."

Anne retreated deeper into the chair. She pulled her parka closed and crossed her arms the way she had the other night.

"We didn't want the same things. He was happy to spend the rest of his life managing a hotel. I didn't, and still don't feel ready to be a homemaker or a housewife."

She pulled a bottle out of her pocket and placed it forcefully on the table. Calvados.

"Is this the bottle you used on Charon?"

"Yes, but it's more than that. It's the symbol of a different life. It's part of my dream. It represents freedom. I've never been farther than New York City. Maybe that's why I liked Martin. He's educated, he travels, and he's lived in foreign countries. He introduced me to Calvados." She lifted the bottle reverently and slipped it into her coat pocket. "And a hundred other things that I might never have had the chance to experience."

"So you're not in love with either Joe Madera or Martin Charon?"

Anne's brow furrowed, and the glow in her eyes almost drowned in a swelling of tears. Her face grew hard and the tears receded.

"I guess I did love Joe a long time ago. We were hardly ever apart, but in the end I discovered that I needed more than he could give me."

"When did you discover that?"

"The realization started to hit me when we painted Martin's house. I became friends with him. I didn't tell you how I met him, did I?"

Niall shook his head.

———

"We met at the cemetery. His parents' grave is near my parents' grave. I was putting fresh flowers on their grave one day, and he stopped me as I was getting back into my work truck. He told me he just bought a house and was looking to have it painted. I gave him a card. A week later he called for an estimate."

Listening to her, Niall felt the hunger again. It thrilled and frightened him. I shouldn't be feeling this, he kept thinking, but he couldn't help himself.

"We did a great job on his house. He liked it so much, he gave us a bottle of Calvados. I loved it and learned all I could about the Pays d'Auge. Do you know about Normandy?"

Niall didn't want to tell her he'd been there a number of times because it might break her talking streak. "Not really," he lied.

"One of these days I'm going to go there. I'll fly to Paris and then I'll drive or take a bus to a town called Honfleur. Martin told me there's a store there that sells only Calvados; the walls are lined with hundreds, – well, maybe dozens – of different types. Or maybe I'll just visit one of the local farmers and find the perfect bottle."

Her story made Niall feel bad that he took his life for granted. He'd been born in Ireland and had spent every summer there from his eighth birthday onward. He'd traveled around Europe, spoke Irish, French, Latin, some Greek and been schooled in the old Gaelic poetic traditions by his father and his uncle Ciarán. He'd hardly used any of it.

"I've been studying French," Anne said, breaking his dream.

"How well do you speak?"

"Not as well as Martin, but I think I can get by."

"Do you think Martin could have done that to Sara?"

"Not a chance. Martin's very particular about his clothes. He might scrub someone to death, but he would never leave them stuffed in a closet full of his pressed shirts and pants." She shuddered. "It must have been someone else. It could have been one of the men who came to Martin's or this Billy Ananda. Where did the Sergeant have to go for the water?"

"Not far, he'll be back soon."

They sat silently for a few minutes.

Mettler returned, carefully balancing a small tray with two glasses of water and a cup of tea in his huge right hand, and wearing a silly grin.

"All that talk of chai made me want a cup of tea." He handed Anne a glass of water and when he was putting the other one in front of Niall, his grin disappeared. He cocked his head. "Can I talk to you outside for a moment, sir?"

Niall's mood changed from mild amusement to concern when he saw the look on his face.

"Excuse me, Anne. We'll be back in a moment."

He followed Mettler into the hallway. The sergeant walked around him and pulled the office door closed behind them, then positioned himself with his back to the glass door.

"What's up, Anthony?"

"We just received word about an explosion and fire out on Durer way."

"Maxwell Good's place?"

"I'm afraid so, sir."

"Shit! Is he hurt?"

"He's been burned, but not badly. Apparently, Joe Madera was killed."

Niall looked over Mettler's shoulder through the glass window to see Anne rummaging through the files on his desk.

"Do you think it odd that as soon as she leaves her house we find a body, and then a short time after she leaves Good's we have another one, sir?"

"I was at Maxwell Good's last night; he's nobody's fool. Anne is as unlikely to have planted an explosive device at his place as she was to drag someone to her bedroom and shoot him in the head. How do you think she'll react when I tell her about Madera?"

"She seems overly emotional," Mettler commented.

"Get over there and see what you can find out. I'll be right behind you."

Mettler hurried down the corridor.

Niall looked through the glass again. Anne was reading a file. He opened the door. She closed the folder quickly and leaned casually against his desk.

"Did you find anything of interest in your file?"

"I only wanted to know what it said. I didn't break any more laws, did I? I hope the news wasn't too serious. You look worried."

Niall didn't want to tell her about Madera. She was just starting to deal with Charon's betrayal and Sara's closet ordeal.

"As a matter of fact I'm afraid it was. I have to leave. Maxwell Good's studio is on fire."

"Max! Was he hurt?" Her knuckles whitened as she gripped the edge of his desk.

"He's on his way to the hospital and from the last report he'll be fine. Why don't you sit down? I have something else to tell you."

Anne's face tightened and grew pale as soon as the words were out of his mouth.

"Someone's dead. Who died?" She slumped into the chair.

"I'm sorry, it was Joe Madera."

"Joe, dead? Oh God! What have I done?"

"Anne, it isn't your fault."

"Oh yes it is. If I had listened to Joe, when I first called him at the hotel, he would still be alive. He wanted me to talk to the police, but I couldn't be bothered. I was too tired. He helped me anyway, and now he's dead."

A tear ran down her cheek. Niall handed her a box of Kleenex from his desk drawer. He placed his hand on her shoulder.

"Don't!" She recoiled from his touch. "I don't deserve to be comforted." Then she lifted her head and looked into his eyes. "I'm sorry. I didn't mean anything. Everyone I know gets hurt or dies."

He watched her wipe away her tears. "I really am sorry about your friend, but I have to go. You can stay here while I look at the warehouse, or if you feel strong enough, you can come with me and we can finish talking on the way."

"I think I'd prefer that. There are a few more things I should tell you."

"Good, I hoped you'd say that."

* * *

CHAPTER IX

Niall's mind raced through the events since Friday night. Now, two people were dead and two were in the hospital. Who was doing all this? What was he not seeing?

"I parked Maxwell's Rolls a few blocks from here," she said, as they reached his plain gray car.

"You can leave it there for now. What haven't you told me?"

She hesitated. "When I first went into Martin's house, there were two bags of tea in the middle of the kitchen floor – not tea bags, but large canvas-covered ones with one- and five-pound packages inside. They're the kind he imports. I've seen them before. I even went with him to the clearinghouse at the airport to pick some bags up once. Anyway, I tripped over them in the dark. I thought it was a body. When you came into the kitchen I was looking for them, but they weren't there."

Niall mentally reviewed the technician's report. "There weren't any bags of tea on the list. Is it possible someone could have come into the house after you left the kitchen? Did you hear any sounds?"

"Maybe, I don't know. I'm not sure. I took Sara into the bathroom and then called the police, but that only took a minute. I went back into the bathroom and stayed with Sara. The shower was running most of the time. She was crying, and with the water running, I don't know if I would have heard anyone."

As the car wove in and out of traffic with its lights flashing, Niall wondered about the bags of tea. Why didn't Anne tell him earlier? What else was she not telling him? He glanced at her. A tear rolled down her face and she swiped at it with the sleeve of her parka. What the hell was he thinking? He was falling for a woman whose greatest goal was to go to Normandy to buy a bottle of Calvados, a woman who ran from everyone who cared for her and caused havoc wherever she went. He pulled into the long row of warehouses.

"Can I go see Sara when we're finished?" She pointed toward the smoke.

His mind said no but his lips said, "Of course you can. In fact, I'll bring you to the hospital, myself."

Shit! What was he doing? A part of him didn't want to let any opportunity to be with her slip between his fingers. He knew his motives were completely wrong, and that he was rationalizing his actions as part of the job. Maggie, why did you have to leave me? His heart pounded.

Patrol units and fire engines were scattered across from where they parked. Hoses crisscrossed the area. Ice had already formed on the ground and around the fire hydrants. Firefighters ran in and out of the warehouse. The police tried to control a small group of locals worried that the fire would spread. Two ambulances with EMTs were parked a short distance away from the engines. He took a deep breath to help clear his head and slipped a cassette into the tape deck sitting next to him.

"What are you doing?" Anne asked. She'd already put her hand on the door handle.

"I'm carrying out a ritual I started several years ago."

He turned to her as the voice of a woman singing a melancholy air filled the car. Anne put her hands in her lap. They stared at each other until he became uncomfortable and looked away.

"It's beautiful," Anne said.

"Traditional Irish. It helps me gather my thoughts before I dive into the kind of wild activity like you see over there. Sometimes I see something that helps me find the solution sooner rather than later. Do you see that green Honda over there?" He pointed toward one of the buildings farther up Durer Way. "Do you recognize it?"

The car was visible for only a second and then it vanished in the smoke swirling between the buildings.

"No."

There wasn't time to leave her with an already busy Mettler and lose the chance to discover who was driving the car that kept appearing at murder scenes.

"Put your seat belt on, and don't get out when I stop the car. Maybe we'll find your friend Martin."

They broke through the wall of smoke created by Maxwell's life's work burning and sped down a maze of narrow driveways, losing sight of the Honda twice. Its driver obviously knew the warehouse area, and Niall began to feel as if they were being led. He called for additional units. Anne grabbed his arm; her hold was distracting but he didn't want her to let go.

They turned a corner. Dead end. The green Honda sat motionless and empty, its driver's door open, framed against a large garage door of almost the same color. Niall pulled to within a few feet of the car and stopped. He called in their position, pushed open his door, and turned to Anne. Her eyes were open wide but she wasn't panicked.

"Don't get out of the car."

He peeled her hand from his arm, and stepped into the cold blue afternoon. He slipped his Glock 34 from under his jacket and walked cautiously toward the Honda, all the while keeping his weapon trained on it. He saw a slight movement out of the corner of his right eye and automatically turned his head to see what or who was moving but didn't see anything. The low-riding afternoon sun cast shadows in all the driveways. The movement could have been a shadow or maybe he was just jumpy.

Niall glanced back at Anne. She fidgeted in her seat.

Where had the driver gone? He opened the Honda's front door, looked inside, and then scanned the warehouses a second time. Niall caught another movement at the side of the same warehouse and walked in that direction with his weapon ready.

Anne banged on the windshield. He waved at her to be quiet. She pushed open the car door. A shot rang out and the window next to her head exploded into a thousand pieces.

Niall ran to the car and threw himself over her, expecting a second shot. The impact of his body sent her headfirst back into the vehicle. He reached past her and grabbed the microphone.

"10-13 officer needs assistance shots fired on Picasso Street at Warehouse Row." He dropped the microphone to the floor.

"Are you all right?" he asked Anne.

She was covered with glass fragments, but didn't appear hurt.

"I felt it go by my head." She put her hand on his cheek. "Was it really a bullet?"

Her cool hand felt good but a rage took hold of him. "Of course it was. What the hell's wrong with you? Why don't you listen to anyone? Didn't I tell you to –?" He stopped himself as her tears started to flow. Shit! Just what I need. "Don't move." He pushed himself off her and crouched behind the car door. "Did you see where the shot came from or who shot at you?"

"By the garage, I think."

Someone must have been over there. Both of them had seen the same movements. The shooter could be anywhere now. His best move was to stay with her until help arrived.

"It's strange being shot at," she said.

You're strange. What had he been thinking? She looked like Maggie but so what? She wasn't Maggie. Maybe he should be searching for her brain instead of for a killer. There was still no movement and no sound, except for Anne's breathing and the grumbling of his empty stomach.

Niall rose slowly to a standing position. He kept his weapon trained in the direction the shot had come from but scanned the spaces and doorways along that row of brightly painted warehouses.

Anne remained prone on the front seat. "I wanted to see what was in the car," she said.

Niall ignored her.

A car screeched to a halt behind them. Mettler jumped out.

"Are you all right, sir?"

He nodded. "Start checking by that warehouse with the blue door, and then have the units seal off the area. Tell them to question anyone they find on foot. We'll check each and every building until we catch the shooter."

Additional units arrived and officers swarmed over the complex checking the doorways and passageways. The sound of a helicopter flying overhead, and the chatter from police radios cluttered what was left of the afternoon peace.

"Can I get up now?" Anne asked.

"Yes."

Why had there been only one shot? The shooter could have gotten off two or three before Niall reached Anne?

"I don't understand what's going on," she said. Her eyes had the same glazed appearance as the other night.

He turned to her. "Someone just tried to kill you."

She shook her head. Pieces of safety glass dropped around her feet. "Why? What did I do that's so terrible? Why would he try to shoot me?"

Niall stepped back. Let me count the reasons for you, he thought. "What makes you sure it was a male?"

She wiped the remnants of tear from her cheek. "You said it was a man driving the car."

He didn't trust her. The entire situation was out of hand. His stomach growled in agreement.

Mettler walked over to them. "We haven't found anyone, sir."

"Find out who owns these warehouses and if any of them are occupied now. Send for forensics and tow trucks for both cars. See if they can find the bullet in the dashboard, and run the license plates to see who owns the Honda. It sounded like a small caliber handgun. See if there are any shell casings by that red door. You know what to do."

"I've already done all that, sir. There are several officers searching the driveway, but there's nothing so far. The car's owner is Jimmy Ramdas; he registered it only two weeks ago."

The dead man in Anne's bedroom had a car and the killer took it. Why hadn't he followed his instinct the other morning and stopped it?

"O.K., I'm going to have a look at Maxwell Good's place, and then I'm taking Anne to the hospital so she can make all better with Sara."

Mettler lowered his voice. "Anne, sir?"

"Don't start again, Anthony. I'm going to talk to Sara Collins again and then Maxwell Good."

"Yes, sir."

"Call, to make sure there is an officer with each of them. Let me know if you find anything. I'll take your car, and meet you at the office."

"Right, sir. There's one more thing."

Niall pulled Mettler away from where Anne stood.

"I hope you don't intend to tell me there's another body."

Mettler laughed. "No, sir, it's a bit more serious than that. It's the Chief. He heard about the explosion and wants to talk to you."

"How do you hear about these things before me?"

"I have private sources, sir." Mettler grinned.

It wasn't unusual for the Chief to want to speak with him. Their friendship went back to Niall's military police days, and he knew the Chief trusted him implicitly. A sense of guilt edged its way into his mind and took a place next to the hunger he'd been feeling. Was he letting everyone down?

"I don't suppose you would share these sources with me?"

"Then they wouldn't be private, would they?"

"I'll talk to the Chief. Clean up here, and I'll meet you at the office. We'll have to find a safe place to keep Anne until we get some answers. I have two more jobs for you. Check the Long

Arms motel. If you find the Indian man Anne told us about, ask him to come in to answer a few questions."

"You mean Doctor Prabdha, sir?"

"Exactly. The second is to look for two large bags of tea. Anne told me she saw them when she first arrived at Charon's house, but they were gone when I was questioning her in the kitchen."

"Where should I look?

"Maybe your private sources will be able to tell you. I'll see you soon."

"Be careful, sir. I think she might be hazardous to your health," Mettler said as Niall started to walk back to Anne.

"Very funny."

Anne left a trail of glass shards in her wake. She stopped before getting in to Mettler's car, took off her coat, removed the bottle of Calvados from the pocket, and then shook the coat until all the loose glass had fallen to the ground. Niall waited. She must know more. She'd seen something at Charon's house. He'd said something she'd forgotten to tell them. Were there gems in the tea? She might still be holding back on him. Were there really two sacks of tea or was she lying?

"We're going to have to find a place for you to stay until Mr. Charon appears. I don't think it's safe for you to run around in the open."

Niall started the engine and began to drive through the maze of police vehicles. The flashing lights on the multicolored buildings faded quickly as they turned the corner.

"I feel like I'm in hell," she said as they turned onto the Route 7 and headed back to town. "I can't stop wondering if Joe's death was my fault."

"You can't take responsibility for everyone's life. Joe helped you because he wanted to help you. Maxwell Good helped because he owed Joe a favor. I'm helping because it's my job."

Anne slid down in her seat, silent and withdrawn. He'd said the wrong thing. His professional tone had made his words sound distant and uncaring.

He felt another twinge of conscience.

* * *

CHAPTER X

The fire was out when they arrived at Maxwell Good's studio. Niall left Anne in the car with an officer keeping an eye on her. He looked over the smoldering ruins; he didn't really expect to find anything, but he never knew.

The remnants of the loft stairway dangled, the rice paper screens around the platform were blackened skeletons, and Maxwell Good's circle of paintings lay in a wet and smoldering pile. Niall remembered Anne lying in the bed and then recalled the feeling of lying on top of her, but shook the image from his head. Anne was trouble. And she wasn't Maggie.

Firefighters still moved about the interior, dowsing hot spots. Niall knew most of them; several volunteered that it was a suspicious event. The arson investigator was already at work in the rear of the warehouse.

The coroner was just bagging Joe Madera's body. The front of which was badly burned, though the back was in remarkably good condition. Niall recognized the unburned sections of the shirt as the one he'd seen Madera wearing a few hours ago. Niall turned from the body and made his way through the debris to where PJ Malloney, the arson investigator, worked several feet away. He squatted next to a mound of plastic and metal containers.

"What's it look like, PJ?" Niall didn't expect much of an answer. PJ wasn't big on words.

"Definitely got yourself a homicide. Amateur stuff, though. Plenty of accelerant, so I'm surprised the explosion wasn't bigger. I'll send you a copy of the report."

Niall thanked him, then left, passing the coroner's men carrying the body bag outside.

"Life is too short," Maggie had repeated to him near the end. She was right.

He didn't speak to Anne as he drove them away from the warehouses. Dark clouds dotted the horizon. The incredibly sunny day might turn into a cloudy afternoon – or the snowstorm the weather people had been predicting. He glanced at Anne and for a second he saw Maggie napping next to him, her eyes barely open, her lips relaxed and slightly apart. Anne wasn't Maggie. His stomach growled.

"I have to find something to eat. It's about a twenty-minute ride to the hospital. Maybe we'll pass someplace that's open on the way."

"You're in charge." Anne's voice was a dull monotone. Was she withdrawing deeper into shock and self-pity or was she just sullen? He didn't really know her.

She slid as far down as the seat belt would allow and closed her eyes.

"Did Martin say where he'd been for the last three days?" Niall asked.

Anne opened her eyes and gave him a strange look. "What are you, a mind reader?"

"I don't understand," he replied.

"I was just trying to remember if he told me where he'd been since Wednesday. How'd you do that?"

"Pure coincidence." He was astonished but pleased. "What else were you thinking?"

"About my conversation with Martin. He never explained about Sara, and I didn't give him time to finish."

"Try piecing it together. What happened after the phone call from the Doctor?" Niall prompted.

"I put the phone down. Martin begged me to let him stay at the house. He touched my hand, and I pulled away." She straightened from her slumped position. "We heard a loud noise from the backyard that sounded like someone knocking over garbage cans. I could tell Martin didn't want to go check it out, but he went anyway. He looked through the window, then went outside. The kitchen was freezing from the cold air coming through the broken windowpane. I needed to distract myself so I cut a piece of cardboard, covered the broken pane, and taped it in place. I was still angry with Martin and Sara. I couldn't stop thinking of them together and suddenly felt I couldn't stay there anymore, so I decided to leave. I went upstairs, grabbed a few things, jumped into my car and drove away. God, I forgot about my car. I must have a million dollars worth of parking tickets."

"Your car has been towed for safekeeping," Niall told her. "Do you remember hearing anything else? Did you see Martin Charon again?"

Anne shifted. The more she talked, the straighter she sat. "The only noises I remember were the sounds of breaking glass, the bottle hitting his head, the phone ringing, and the backyard noise. But as I drove away, I thought I saw someone watching me from my bedroom window."

"Try to visualize the watcher. Was it Charon?"

Anne shrugged. "It was too dark. And I had only an impression that someone was there so it could have been my imagination. All I know is that I was happy to be out the house."

Niall's hunger pains were getting stronger than before and made it difficult for him to concentrate; he cursed himself for not eating lunch.

He knew the only place to eat near the hospital was a greasy fast food restaurant as famous for its cockroaches as for its grease. Niall parked in the same spot as the day before.

"My parents died here," Anne said. I was four but back then the building was as white as a nurse's uniform."

She jumped out and strode directly to the entrance.

"Wait a second," he called, but she was gone.

He locked the car, ran into the emergency room, and caught a glimpse of her as she slipped out another door and into the main hospital where signs pointed to the cafeteria. Niall followed Anne down hallways to the cafeteria. The medium-sized dining room was clean, but worn. Several people sat around sipping drinks, but he didn't see anyone eating. The fluorescent lighting gave everyone a sickly pallor.

He watched Anne grab a tray and move down the line. The salads looked wilted, and the sandwiches soggy and gray, but he took a tuna salad sandwich. Anne opted for a bowl of red Jell-O and a container of milk. He didn't bother to ask why she hadn't waited for him; it would have been a waste of time. He'd have liked to lock her up as a material witness but he knew he wouldn't.

Anne held her tray toward him. "They looked like the least dangerous items. Do you think this Jell-O could be from the same batch I had twenty-five years ago?"

Niall smiled. Anthony wouldn't touch anything in the place except a cup of tea, and berated Niall every time he popped in here for a quick bite, but Niall liked their tuna sandwiches and always got one.

She paid for her food, and walked to an empty table. Niall paid for his sandwich, then sat next to her. She opened her container of milk and poured it on the Jell-O, until there were only see two small red islands swaying in an ocean of white, then she looked up with a sad smile.

"What's wrong now?" he asked.

"It reminds me of my father and mother. Mom used to make it like this all the time. God, I haven't thought about it in years."

She lowered her head; a tear fell into the milk.

Her emotions struck too close to home for Niall. He'd always managed to keep his professional distance on cases, but this woman did something to him.

He unwrapped his sandwich and took a bite. The food sent a surge of energy through his body.

"We'll go up to Sara's room when we're done. When we've finished speaking with her and Maxwell Good, we'll go back to the office and find you a safe place to stay while I try to put all the pieces together."

Anne seemed to have pushed her melancholy aside as she enjoyed her soupy concoction, scooping up the last vibrating chunk of Jell-O. Her mood had changed a dozen times since she'd walked into his office two hours earlier. It didn't inspire confidence. He wondered what would happen when she faced Sara.

"Shall we go?" he asked.

She stood, straightened her clothes, and then picked another shard of glass out of her hair. "I'm ready."

Sara's room was on the second floor. Niall thought he might ask if Maxwell Good could be put in an adjacent room.

"Does Sara know Joe is dead?" Anne asked as they left the cafeteria.

"I can't imagine anyone would have told her."

"Can I tell her?"

"I don't think so, but let me think about it," Niall replied. Giving news like that was something most people avoided, so it was strange that Anne wanted to do it.

The first-floor tiles were worn from all the passing feet in the years since the hospital opened. The smell of disinfectant clung in his nostrils as they passed through the hallways and into the elevator. Anne appeared tenser after the elevator doors closed.

She stepped out first, then turned and pointed down the hallway. "What's she doing here?"

Niall saw Flemming standing in front of Sara's room. "Keeping an eye on Sara," he replied.

Anne mumbled under her breath. Niall ignored it.

When they reached Flemming, the women nodded at each other but neither spoke. Niall took Flemming aside, but kept his eye on Anne, who remained fixed in front of Sara's door.

"I want you to speak with the head nurse. Ask her to arrange to have Maxwell Good put in the room next to Sara. It will be easier for us to keep an eye on the both of them if they're together," he told Flemming. He saw Anne take a deep breath and turn the handle but the door didn't open.

"Is the door supposed to be locked?" she asked.

Niall looked at Flemming.

She said, "The doors don't have locks, sir. I checked her an hour ago and she was fine. She said she wanted to take a nap, and I've been here since."

Niall tried the door. Something was blocking it. He knocked. "Sara. It's Lieutenant O'Huiginn. Open the door."

They waited a few seconds, but there was no response.

"Find someone to open this door," Niall told Flemming.

"Yes, sir." She walked briskly toward the nurses' station.

Anne banged on the door again, harder than Niall had, but there was still no response. Niall watched her but did nothing. She was distraught and needed to let it out; his stopping her would only postpone it. If Sara were asleep, the banging should wake her; if she weren't... Niall didn't want to think that she might be dead.

Suddenly Anne started hammering on the door as hard as she could. Several people looked out of nearby rooms as Anne continued banging on the door.

Flemming ran back to them from the nurses' desk.

"What's the matter with her?"

"Did you find someone to open the door?" Niall asked, ignoring her question.

"The nurse called building maintenance, but it's going to be a few minutes. Shouldn't we stop her?"

"No. I bet she hasn't let go in a long time."

Eventually, weariness caused Anne to stop. There was still no sign of any maintenance people. Niall touched Anne's shoulder. She looked at him with sadness and fatigue.

A sound behind the door caught their attention. Anne moved aside. Niall reached inside his jacket and placed his hand on his automatic as the door opened.

Sara stood there looking sleepy, somewhat ruffled and confused. "Why were you banging so much?"

"Why did you block the door? Officer Flemming was stationed right outside." Niall pushed past her into the room. Anne followed.

The room was cold. Had the window been open? It was closed now.

"I was afraid to sleep with the door unlocked," Sara replied.

"Why did you open the window if you were afraid?"

"We're on the second floor. Who would come in the window?" She looked better than she had the day before. She wasn't as pale and had pulled her hair into a ponytail.

Anne, on the other hand, looked haggard. Niall caught himself comparing the women and went to sit on the edge of the bed. The sheets were as cold as the room. A sweet floral scent from the bouquets drifted to him in waves; the smell reminded him of Maggie's funeral.

Sara moved closer to Anne, smiling nervously. Sara appeared to want to hug Anne but seemed afraid of how she would react. Niall decided to break the stalemate.

"I appreciate your concerns, Miss Collins. However, I must ask you not to block the door, and please leave the window closed. It's for your safety. There will be an officer outside your door until you leave the hospital. I'll leave now, so you two can have a few minutes alone. I'm sure you have a lot to say to each other. When I return, I'll have a few more questions for you."

Anne whispered to him, "You never told me if I could tell her about Joe."

"Don't say anything until I return." When she frowned in mock displeasure, he added, "I'm serious." He walked out.

"Even in a hospital people like excitement," Flemming said to him.

"Did you do what I asked?"

"Yes, sir. They're bringing Mr. Good up now. The nurse said his hands were burned and he inhaled some smoke, but he'll be as good as new in a few weeks."

"I want you to keep a close eye on both of these people. You have a picture of Martin Charon, don't you?"

"Yes, sir."

"If you see him, arrest him."

He walked down the hall and sat on a fake leather-covered chair only a short distance away. He wanted to allow Anne and Sara some time alone to resolve their differences but not too long.

A minute later two attendants wheeled Maxwell Good down the corridor and into the room next to Sara's. A doctor named Whitely led the small entourage, then stepped back until Good was safely in his room.

"Was that outbreak more of your doing, Lieutenant?"

"It seemed necessary, but I'm sorry if it caused anxiety in any of your patients."

"This is a hospital, not a police station. We're happy to cooperate with the authorities, but we can't have the patients being disturbed."

Niall jumped to his feet.

"Listen, first I want you to know that we truly appreciate the hospital's willingness to assist us. Second, I don't know if you're having a bad day, but I am. I have two dead people and two more in the hospital. Now, if you have no objection, I'd like to have a few words with Mr. Good."

Dr. Whitely recovered quickly. "You'll have to wait a few more minutes. I want to be certain Mr. Good is comfortable." He marched into the room and closed the door behind him, but not before giving Niall a satisfied grin.

"You shouldn't have to take that crap from him, sir. I'll bet he doesn't even live in town," Flemming said.

"He's the doctor, and this is his hospital."

Niall paced for a few minutes until he decided on a plan of action, even though he wasn't sure it was a good one.

He knocked on Sara's door, then entered without waiting for a response. "We need to continue. You two will have plenty of time to talk later." Sara used a tissue to wipe her tears; Anne's face was tight and pale, but without tears.

Sara sat on the edge of the bed. "I'm ready now, Lieutenant."

"Thank you. Have you seen or spoken to a Dr. Ramchander Prabdha?"

"No. Who's he?"

"Do you have any idea why you were left naked in the closet?"

"No, I don't." She blushed.

"Miss Collins, Sara, do you want to catch the people who killed Joe Madera?" He said it without changing his tone and watched surprise appear on both faces.

"Excuse me? Did you say Joe is dead? You're joking, right?" Sara tried to smile.

Niall had seen that kind of smile a dozen times. It was a combination of shock and denial when people didn't know how to respond. It was honest but the odd smile disappeared when Sara saw Anne's face.

"Is it true, Annie? Joe's dead? How could that be? I don't understand." She turned toward the window and searched the darkness.

"Yes, it's true. He died about two hours ago. Please help any way you can, Sara," Anne said.

"Anne, I...I'm so sorry. I don't know what to say. I can't believe it. It's like a dream that doesn't end."

Sara hugged Anne, who looked drained, almost defeated. Sara sounded sincere, but something about her reaction bugged Niall, what was it? She was definitely surprised. Doubts about both women and about the way he was handling the situation arose, making him uneasy. Could they be playing him?

"May we continue, Sara?" he asked.

Sara's tight hold on Anne loosened.

"Yes, certainly. I'll do whatever I can to help."

"Do you remember seeing two large bags of tea in the kitchen – or anywhere else in the house – last Wednesday?"

Sara closed her eyes and thought for a second. "No."

Anne looked surprised. The sacks could have arrived when Sara was in the closet and then been removed, but she should have heard anyone come into the house the same way she'd heard Anne arrive. On the other hand, Sara might have been too involved with Martin to notice the bags.

"It might be a good time for you to visit Mr. Good while I finish up here, Anne," he said. "He's been moved to the room next door."

"Why is Maxwell here?" Sara asked Anne.

"He was hurt in the explosion that killed Joe. He's being treated for burns." She walked to the door, then turned and added, "I'll call the Dolentzes about rescheduling the job. Take care of yourself."

Niall held the door for her.

"Don't go anywhere. I'll be over soon." He smiled at her and closed the door.

"Anne doesn't look good," Sara said.

"You've both been through terrible ordeals over the last few days. Did she tell you someone shot at her an hour ago?"

"Oh my God! She didn't say anything about that. What happened?"

"I don't have the time to explain, but I'll tell you all about it as soon as I can. Do you remember seeing an older model green Honda parked at or near Martin's house?"

Sara went back to her bed and propped herself against the pillows.

"No, but I'm not much for noticing things. Anne is the observant one. I'm more internal."

Niall walked to the window. Sara had looked toward the window when he told her about Joe's death, and he wondered why. It was already dark, but he could see the roof, flat and black, stretching out before him.

Sara spoke. "Do you know if I was raped? The doctors and nurses haven't told me anything."

He turned to her. She looked more relaxed than Anne. He felt certain she had had sex, but had she agreed to it or had it been rape?

"They don't know for sure."

A crash from the hallway grabbed their attention; another bang and the sound of Flemming yelling followed it.

Niall rushed to the door, pulled it open. Flemming stood a few yards down the hallway. A food cart had been knocked over and the unhappy attendant scraped spilled food onto a tray.

"Flemming, what's all the commotion?"

"Anne Tadmore ran out of the room and down the corridor, sir. I yelled for her to stop but she kept going down the hall, and barreled right into that cart. She just went out the door at the end of the hallway."

Niall was already running. "Don't let either of them out of their rooms," he yelled back at her.

When he reached the far end of the hallway and heard Flemming saying loudly, "Shit! Shit! Shit!"

He felt the same way. Why was Anne running again? She must be crazy. He paused in the stairwell to listen and heard the sound of a door closing below him. He took the stairs three at a time until he burst out on the first floor and stumbled over a young boy in a wheelchair. The doorway was at a hallway intersection. He didn't see Anne's green parka in front of him, so he quickly looked to his right and caught a glimpse as she ran out a door. Niall sprinted the length of the hallway and into the darkened streets. She was gone.

He yelled into the emptiness of the cold night, "Maggie, come back."

* * *

CHAPTER XI

Her name hung in the still night air. Niall inhaled sharply as he realized that he'd been mentally transported back to his endless trips to this hospital with Maggie. A wave of sadness and loss radiated from the center of his chest to his throat.

Niall took a deep breath and let it out slowly. He raised his eyes toward the sky; the brightest winter stars twinkled a lonely indecipherable message. He brought his eyes and himself back to earth. The street was calm and silent.

Perhaps he'd been in denial about Maggie's death for the last year. Although there was nothing he could have done to keep her alive, he'd never felt so powerless; after she died, he'd felt angry.

He'd lost his father and then Maggie, but he would be damned if he'd allow someone to harm Anne. Niall reached into his pocket, pulled out his cell phone, and dialed Mettler's number.

"Anthony, I lost Anne Tadmore."

"Really, sir?" Mettler responded quietly but Niall detected some glee, perhaps because it hadn't been him who'd lost her.

"Yes, really! Put out an APB; she's wanted in connection with the two homicides. I want the streets around St. Mary's Hospital flooded with any available units until we find her. She's on foot, so she can't get too far."

"I'll get right on it. Is there anything else?"

"No, that's it. I should be back within a half-hour. Let me know if they find her."

"Yes, sir."

Niall surveyed the street for another minute, but a gust of cold wind pushed him toward the door. Why had she run? Someone had just tried to shoot her – did she have a death wish? Flemming was pacing back and forth along the second floor corridor like a prisoner waiting for a verdict. Her jaw was clenched, her shoulders were hunched.

Niall told her, "If either Miss Collins or Mr. Good attempts to leave you have my permission to use whatever force is necessary to stop them."

"Yes, sir," she replied, immediately looking less tense.

Niall went directly to Maxwell Good's door, knocked, and walked in. Good didn't look too bad considering his harrowing afternoon. His purple hair was singed in a few places; his hands were covered with bandages and rested on pillows.

"Did you find Anne?" he asked.

Niall shook his head.

"It's my fault she ran," Good said.

"What happened?"

"She was crying when she came in. I told her we'd catch Joe's killer, that I have money to hire the best detectives to find out who was behind the explosion. I pushed her and pushed her about finding the person responsible for Joe's death. I was so caught up in my own self-righteousness that I hadn't realized she was so fragile. You should have seen her this morning she seemed so cocky and full of life," he sighed. "Then in the middle of my tirade, she blurted out that her mother had died in this very room.

I was still so caught up in my own babble that I didn't recognize how upset she was. Anyway, the more I chattered at her, the more upset she became, and then she ran out the door."

"Did she tell you someone shot at her after the explosion?"

Good shook his head.

"What happened after Anne left your studio, – and how did Mr. Madera come to be there?"

Good tried to scratch his face with his bandaged right hand. "Joe called me right after you released him. He said he'd had a hard night, needed to make some decisions, and would like to discuss his possibilities with me. I figured I still owed him, so I told him I'd be delighted to chat with him – besides, I like company. Anne was getting ready to leave about the time he called and he arrived an hour after she left. We talked for a while and then went for a walk. It was pretty cold, so we only stayed out for about a half-hour. When we returned, my studio door was unlocked. I said we should call the police, but Joe stormed right into the studio to have a look for himself and I followed him.

"The studio looked undisturbed, and I thought maybe I'd forgotten to lock the door. Joe was already down at the other end. He motioned for me to call the police because he'd noticed the door leading to the garage was open. He tiptoed to the door and picked up one of my hammers on the way. I went to the phone and started to dial when I saw him slip into the garage. I heard glass breaking. I told the operator what was going on, then listened again and heard another loud crash that sounded like the outside garage door slamming closed. I called to Joe, but he didn't answer. I picked up a piece of wood and had just put my hand on the door when the whole place blew up. The explosion sent me about fifteen feet with the door on top of me. The firemen say the steel door saved my life and I was the luckiest person they'd run across in a while." He gave Niall a sad smile. "Can you believe that?"

"Do you remember seeing an older model green Honda around when you went for your walk with Joe?"

Good tried scratching at his face again without apparent success. "A car like that was parked in front of my neighbor's garage. He hates anyone blocking his door."

"What do you remember after the explosion?"

"I think I blacked out for a few minutes. When the shock wore off, I was still under the door. My right hand felt numb and my ears were ringing. I struggled to pull myself out from under the door and screamed for Joe. The studio was filling with smoke, and the flames were spreading to my canvases. I continued calling Joe's name as I crawled around looking for him." He gaze challenged Niall. "I knew he would do the same thing for me. Well, the next thing I remember was one of your policemen pulling me out into the roadway. The officer went back in to find Joe, but the smoke was too thick and toxic. He came out hacking and coughing a few minutes later, so all we could do was wait for the fire engines to arrive."

Niall had sat motionless all during Good's story, but now he felt the need to move around. He walked to the window and looked out at the same roof that Sara had glanced at a short time ago; it bothered him, the way she glanced to the window when he told her about Madera.

"You must think me a coward," Good said.

The statement surprised Niall.

"On the contrary, I think Joe Madera was foolhardy; he'd still be alive if he'd listened to you. The right thing was to wait outside for people trained to handle those kinds of situations. I'd like to know what he talked to you about before the explosion."

"I suppose it doesn't matter now but Joe spilled his guts – or at least I think he did. He wasn't one for being exact. He was vague about Anne, his job, and that woman boss of his."

"Gennifer Bidon?"

"Yup, that's the one. He called her the fire woman."

Niall wondered if he called her that because of her red hair or because she was looking for a hose to put out the fire burning inside her.

"Anyhow, I gather he was doing fine until Sara called him two weeks ago about Martin and Anne. Well, that got him thinking about Anne again, so when she called the other morning he fell completely off the wagon. He told me he'd just spent a miserable night with Gennifer Bidon then later he found out from you that she knew Anne had called him and knew that his boss would make his life miserable. I felt bad for him, but I didn't know what to say. He kept apologizing, but I didn't understand what he was talking about. 'I'm really sorry about everything, Maxwell. I'm really sorry. I hope you can forgive me.' He said it over and over."

"Do you think he was suicidal?"

"No, no way. Joe's not that kind of guy."

"Thanks. That's it for now. Take care of yourself. If you remember anything else, tell one of the officers outside your room to call me."

"I will. I will. And find Anne. I don't want anything to happen to her."

"I'll do my best."

Niall left the room, his head buzzing with images: Anne running away from her house, then down the hospital hall; Maggie in a hospital bed upstairs; Anne's exposed shoulder; Madera's burned face; the dead man in Anne's chair; the two large sacks of tea. The situation just didn't make sense.

The phone was ringing when he walked into his office. He picked it up.

"It's about time, Niall."

"Hey Packy." Chief Pack usually left him alone, but they also usually didn't have this much violent crime in such a short span of time. "I was just about to call you."

"Sure you were. I don't suppose you wanted to tell me you caught the maniac who is running around killing citizens."

"You don't suppose correctly, but we're working on it," Niall replied wryly.

"This is only January, but the manpower and overtime are already burning a deep hole in the budget. I don't want to have to go the city council in September with my hand out."

"I hear you." Niall dropped into his chair and checked the icicle. It was still there.

"Let me know as soon as anything breaks," Packy finished.

Mettler entered the room as Niall hung up. "The Chief isn't happy. The bodies are piling up and so is the pressure," he told him.

"Yes, sir, I'm aware of that. Everyone's looking for Ms. Tadmore. She can't have gotten far. Can I ask how she got away, sir?" After Niall briefed him, he said, "Sounds like the pressure is building up all over the place, and pressure always needs to be released."

Niall hoisted his feet onto the desk. "If we don't find her, I'm afraid we'll have more bodies to explain. She may have friends in the area, so take Sara's phone book and check the addresses, especially if there are any near the hospital."

"I'm on it, sir."

Niall stared at the faded green walls of his office. He wondered if Anne was right about lead paint, and if it might be having a cumulative effect on his thinking. Then again, the whole situation didn't make sense. If they were looking for the gems and if Charon wasn't involved, why didn't his house show signs of a search? Why did they strip Sara and leave her in the closet? Why did they kill Jimmy Ramdas and leave him in the women's house? Niall had also been out of the car long enough for the guy to have a clear shot at him, so why had they shot at Anne? At that moment, he had posed more of threat than Anne did, so it must have been Anne that he or they were after. Why?

A knock on the door brought him back. Herzog stood in the doorway.

"Sorry to bother you, we just got a call about an attempted kidnapping of a woman by three men over on Sussex Avenue, only a few blocks from the hospital; the description sounds like the Tadmore woman."

Niall slid his feet to the floor. "Is that all you've got?"

"The details are sketchy: Three men tried to grab a woman. Three other men attacked them. The perps fled and so did she. We already had several units dispatched to the area to look for her, so we're waiting for them to report in with more information."

"O.K. I'm heading over there." Niall stood and grabbed his heavy winter coat from the rack. "If the report on the explosion or about the Honda comes in, let me know," he said as he left.

He grabbed Mettler on his way to the garage and signed out a car, inserting his favorite cassette. The lamenting tones of The Dark Woman of the Glen filled the car as they pulled into the dark streets. Mettler hummed along with the music and tapped his fingers on his knees.

They turned onto Sussex Avenue as the last notes of the song faded. Patrol cars cruised up and down the side streets, but two blocks ahead, was a small group of units stopped in one place.

Niall pulled up and sat in the car as Mettler jumped out, not seeming to mind the cold that had kept its grip on the region for the last several days. The sub-zero wind didn't seem to bother the neighbors either; they stood in the street gossiping. An area had been marked off with tape and officers moved around inside with flashlights.

Mettler went directly to Boehm, the on-scene supervisor, as the lights swirled in the darkness.

Niall scanned the crowd, but couldn't see them all from the car, so he stepped out and looked around for anyone who might be out of place. A strong gust of wind bit into his face. He buttoned his coat and walked over to the two sergeants.

"Lieutenant." Boehm nodded curtly.

He returned the nod. "I hate to make you start all over, but fill me in on what happened, will you?"

"I hadn't really started yet." Boehm tapped his notebook with his pen. "At about six-thirty several of the residents heard a woman shouting for help. See the old woman upstairs at the window?" He pointed to a third-floor window of the brick building in front of them. "She saw most of what happened through the bare branches of the tree. She said a tall white male with long-ish dark hair got out of a car, then the car drove off. He stood behind the tree trunk over there, waiting." He aimed his pen at a of a huge maple tree. "The guy was only there for a minute or two, and the old woman thought he was relieving himself on the tree. Then down the street came this young woman wearing jeans and a green parka."

"Does this old woman have a name?" Niall asked, sticking his hands in his coat pockets.

"Yes, sir." Boehm glanced at his notes. "Fan O'Halloran. Anyway, the man steps out from behind the tree and starts talking to the girl who Mrs. O'Halloran said looked frightened or nervous. The guy grabbed her by the arm and she started to pull away. Mrs. O'Halloran banged on her window to let the man know someone was watching. Then the car that had just dropped the man off pulled up again. She said two 'foreign-looking' men jumped out, and all three men attempted to drag the screaming woman into the car when three local kids ran up and started beating the guys with bats. The three would-be kidnappers jumped back into the vehicle, and the kids beat the car until it pulled away in a cloud of smoking rubber."

Niall studied the black imprints on the asphalt and the pieces of red and orange plastic mixed with broken glass. "Did she know what make car it was?"

"Just that it was dark-colored. We shouldn't have too hard a time finding the car with all the broken windows and dents."

"Forensics will probably be able to identify the make from all those pieces. What happened after the car left?" Niall asked.

"Mrs. O'Halloran says the woman talked to the three kids for about a minute, and then all four of them walked off down the street. By that time, other people were coming to their windows and out into the street. When we arrived here, she opened her window and yelled down to one of the patrolman."

Boehm wiped his nose with the back of his hand and stomped his foot. His actions reminded Niall of a horse.

"We haven't interviewed all the neighbors. That's all we have so far. I sent a few units to see if they can locate the woman and the three kids. I put out a call to all the local agencies to keep an eye out for the car, too. They'll probably dump it soon," Boehm finished.

"This occurred about thirty minutes ago. Anne and her heroes are on foot," Niall said to no one in particular.

"They couldn't have gone far because we were already patrolling the area when the call came in," Boehm replied.

"The old lady said they were local kids," Mettler pointed out.

"That's exactly what I was thinking. Let's go have a chat in her nice warm apartment, Anthony." He turned to Boehm. "See if any of the neighbors got the license plate number or recognized those kids. Since we haven't found them yet, they must have gone inside somewhere near here. Have the cars continue to cruise the streets, but tell them to turn off those damn lights. They might come back out if the place isn't lit up like a circus."

"Got it." Boehm hurried away.

Niall and Mettler headed toward the brick building.

The warm interior hallway was a relief. They climbed the stairs to the third floor and Mettler knocked on Mrs. O'Halloran's door while Niall waited.

An old woman's voice yelled from the other side of the door. "Who's that trying to break down my door when I'm watching the evening news?"

Mettler put his mouth next to the door and said loudly. "It's the police, Mrs. O'Halloran. We'd like to ask you a few more questions if you don't mind."

The bolt turned and the door opened, revealing a woman about 5 foot 4 inches tall with snow-white hair and blazing blue eyes.

"Jesus, Mary and Joseph, will you look at the size of him – he's as big as a house!" Mrs. O'Halloran slowly bent her neck until she could see all of Mettler.

"Ma'am, I'm Sergeant Mettler and this is Lieutenant O'Huiginn. We'd like to ask you a few more questions about the incident you witnessed a little while ago outside your window. May we come in?"

She studied Niall for a minute. "I suppose the news is right here tonight. The TV will have to wait. Come in and wipe your feet. I don't need you traipsing dirt onto my clean floors. Close the door behind you." She turned and shuffled back into the apartment.

Mettler stepped aside to let Niall go first.

Niall smiled. The woman reminded him of his long-dead grandmother. She wore a heavy white woolen sweater over a rose flower-patterned housecoat. The short hallway was filled with the familiar aroma of freshly baked Irish soda bread mixed with the chemical smells of cleaning fluids and lemon oil. It all reminded him of his childhood and the day his family had left Ireland.

The woman's apartment was spotless. Pieces of well-polished furniture decorated the rooms. Lace doilies covered the arms of the chairs and created a warm, homey atmosphere. They followed Mrs. O'Halloran into the living room. She turned off the TV and sat in a comfortable-looking high-backed chair.

"O'Huiginn? I knew a poet named Niall O'Huiginn from Galway. Are you any relation to him?" She looked up at the men standing in front of her. "Sit down, would you; I'll get a crick in my neck if I have to keep my head bent."

Mettler sat on a plain dark wooden chair that creaked under his weight. Niall removed his overcoat, walked around the glistening coffee table, and sat on the vinyl-covered couch, then answered her question.

"That could have been my father. I doubt if there were too many like him. We came here when I was six years old."

"Well, I knew your father and mother. It is a small world, isn't it? I'm sure we must have met when you were little. I heard your father read several times. It was a shame what happened to him, but I see you turned out well in spite of his misfortune. Look at you, and you're a Lieutenant too. Oh! He was a grand poet in the old tradition. Did you inherit his gift?"

She seemed happy just to have someone to talk to.

"I don't know."

"I'm from Clare myself. Do you have any Irish?" she asked.

"I do."

"When things calm down, you must come over for a cup of tea and soda bread. I'll not take no for an answer. We can see how much we both remember," she said. "I'm humbly grateful for what I have, but I'm alone here, you see. Not too many of my old friends are still around, God bless them and keep them! My son owns this building and lets me live here free, but he's too busy to come and visit. I ask you, is it a nice thing for a son to leave his eighty-three year-old mother alone? You see how it is now, don't you?" She shook her head and smiled at Niall. "Now, what is it you need to know?"

Mettler waited, notebook and pencil in hand.

Mettler said, "Ma'am, the officer you spoke with a little while ago told us you said the young men who helped the woman were from the neighborhood. Can you tell us anything more about them? Do you know where they live?"

"Well now, you see, since I'm alone, *agus ta an aimsir ag cur seaca.*"

Niall nodded as Mettler looked up from his notebook.

"It's been so cold out, Sergeant," she explained, "That I spend a lot of time looking out the window."

Niall glanced at the window where she had set up a straight-backed chair and a small oak table covered with a lace doily. The chair cushions had taken on a curved shape from her many hours of lonely watching. On the table sat a book, two magazines, and a pair of reading glasses.

"Please continue, Mrs. O'Halloran."

"Well you see, I know all the neighbors, their comings and goings and one of the young men you're looking for walks down this street every other day or so. He comes from up toward Long Branch Road and then sometimes, if I sit at the window long enough, I see him going back up that way a few hours later. I'd know him even in the dark, like this evening. I think he might have some relatives living down toward the Boulevard."

"What makes you think that?"

"I've seen him with a young girl and her baby on a few occasions. They're like bookends, the two of them, except she's a girl and he's boy. I see her from time to time walking with a foreign man. I think it's her husband."

Mettler had looked up. "What makes you think he's a foreign man? What kind of foreign man is he?" he asked.

"He looks like he might be from Pakistan, or India, or one of those places in the Middle East. I watch the world news, and I've learned to recognize many people." She seemed satisfied that her knowledge of the world and its happenings finally could be used for something. "God help us, it's changed an awful lot around here in the last ten years."

Niall said, "You told the officer earlier that two of the men who tried to abduct the young woman looked like foreigners. Do you think that they were Pakistanis or Indians also?"

"Well, now that you mention it, I think you're right. Isn't that something?" She raised her right hand to her chin and looked off into the distance, apparently revisiting the event.

"You don't know where the young mother lives then?" Mettler asked.

"I don't get out very often, you see, except to go to mass. I seem to recall when I was on my way to mass one Saturday afternoon – you know I go to the five o'clock mass on Saturday so I don't have to go running out on a cold Sunday morning. Anyway, I remember seeing the same girl a few blocks down, toward the Boulevard." She pointed in the direction of Hohokus Boulevard. "She was coming out of one of those newly renovated buildings. Have you seen them?" she asked Niall.

"Yes, I drive by them quite often. *Go raibh maith agat!* You've been a great help, Mrs. O'Halloran, and we certainly appreciate it. If you remember anything, anything at all, please call me. Here's my card."

"*Níl a bhuíochas ort!* It was nothing at all. When things quiet down, you come back, and we'll refresh our Irish, and talk about poetry and your father. May God save us! It's a pity he died so young."

"I will, and thank you very much."

"What was that she said at the end?" Mettler asked Niall after they left the apartment and walked down a flight of stairs.

"Sort of like, don't mention it."

"You never talk much about your father, sir. I knew he was a poet, but not that he was famous."

"We come from a long line of traditional Irish poets. The language and the knowledge was passed from father to son, father to son, for hundreds of years." Niall spoke in a monotone, as if he were reciting for a teacher.

"Is that why you have the poem on the wall in your office?"

"Yes." Niall stopped and turned to Mettler. "I'd appreciate it if you didn't mention to anyone else about my father and the poetry, Anthony."

"Whatever you want, but I don't understand why. Everyone at the office knows your father was a poet."

"I just don't want to go into it right now." The words came out too forcefully, but it was too late. Mettler had pulled back.

"No problem, sir, it's forgotten."

Niall's stomach twisted. He didn't want to alienate Mettler. He sighed. "I'm sorry, Anthony. There's too much going on right now with the murders, the gems, Anne, and Maggie."

Mettler put his large hand on Niall's shoulder. "Are you sure you want to finish this case, sir?"

Niall smiled at him. "I'm sure – and I'll tell you all about my father and everything else when, as Mrs. O'Halloran said, things quiet down. Is that O.K.?"

Mettler smiled and shrugged, then dropped his hand and continued as if nothing had happened. "What do we do about the loose cannons running around the streets?"

"Resources are spread pretty thin, but I'll see if we can get at least one unmarked car down the street. They'll have to sit and see if Anne comes out of hiding with her new friends. Talk to the people in the street and see if any of the neighbors knows those three kids' names. We can only hope they didn't have a car nearby. In the meantime, we'll have some of the patrol units stay alert for the two Indian men and Charon. Ask the hospitals to keep an eye out for anyone coming in with injuries that might be from a fight; it's a long shot that one was hurt bad enough to need medical attention, but it's worth a try."

"Right, sir, I'll take care of things here and catch a ride back with Boehm."

* * *

CHAPTER XII

N iall walked out of the cold garage and into Herzog at the corridors' crossroads.

"Sorry, L.T."

"No, it was my fault. The case is making me absent-minded," Niall replied, wondering what could make the night worse.

"Cheer up, L.T. It can't be that bad." Herzog added. "By the way, there's someone waiting to see you."

"You don't say. I suppose it would be too much to hope that it's our murderer giving himself up."

"Wouldn't it be nice if they all walked in and confessed," Herzog grinned.

"We'd be out of jobs in no time if the world functioned in a rational manner – and then, what would we do with ourselves?"

"I guess we'd have to learn new trades. I think he does have something to do with your case, though. It's an Indian guy."

"Where is he?"

"Sitting outside your office. He walked in right after you went over to Sussex Avenue."

"Thanks. Anthony should be back soon. Tell him I need him in my office, will you?"

"Sure thing."

Niall enjoyed his walk through the warm corridors; the heat was helping clear his head.

A well-dressed Indian man around sixty years old sat outside his office door; he stood when he saw Niall approaching.

Niall extended his hand. "Dr. Ramchander Prabdha?"

Prabdha hesitated a second, then shook hands. The doctor was a tall man who stood straight and proud.

"Yes. You must be Lieutenant O'Huiginn. I confess to surprise that you know my name." He spoke slowly, and with a thick but controlled Indian accent.

"Anne Tadmore told me about your phone conversation and I knew it was only a matter of time before you showed up around here, one way or another."

"I have been following her adventures in the newspapers. It is unfortunate I did not arrive here a few days sooner. All of the death and destruction might have been avoided."

"Come into my office. It's more comfortable."

Niall pushed open the door and allowed his visitor to enter first. As he hung up his coat, he studied the man. Prabdha seemed relaxed. He sat in the chair in front of Niall's desk and looked around Niall's unimpressive office.

"I see the bureaucracy treats its officials with the same courtesy in this country as they do in mine," he observed.

"I guess I've grown accustomed to it." Niall walked around his desk and sat. "What brings you here, Dr. Prabdha? And what kind of doctor are you?"

"You are quite direct."

Niall didn't respond.

"I am a doctor of Homeopathy. However, I have not practiced for many years." Prabdha fidgeted with his tie's knot and then ran his hand the length of the tie to smooth it. "Occasionally, I do little things for friends and family, but my devotion to the family business has grown to be all-inclusive of my time. As for your first question…" he paused. "It is a long story." He looked uncertain.

"I've had my share of long stories in the last few days, but if yours will help me find out why people are dying, I'd be happy to listen to another one." Niall watched Prabdha intently and noticed that his gaze did not appear to bother him.

"This story is also one of a delicate nature that could have international repercussions, so forgive me for hesitating, but I must be certain of your ability to help. I also require some confidentiality."

Niall raised an eyebrow. "We've had two people murdered and two admitted to the hospital in the last three days. I'm certain there will be more if we don't find out soon what is going on and who is responsible. If your story helps me catch the bad guys, I'll leave out any unnecessary details – but if you don't tell me, I'll make sure everything I find out appears in the papers."

"I see you are a reasonable man and very determined, too. Very well, first I must give you some background information. I live in Padum, a town in the Zaskar Mountains of Kashmir in India."

Mettler announced his arrival with a knock. Niall motioned for him to enter.

"Did I hear you say Zaskar and Kashmir?" Mettler said as he entered. "I was just reading about that region of India."

"Sergeant Mettler, this is Doctor Prabdha, the man who's been calling our two damsels in distress."

"Nice to meet you. Lieutenant, can I talk to you outside a minute?"

"Can't it wait?" Niall was slightly annoyed.

"I don't think so, sir."

"O.K., please excuse us a minute."

Niall rose from his desk, smiled cordially at the doctor. Mettler pulled the door closed and stepped down the hall before they spoke.

"I'm sorry to tell you this, sir, but it seems Ms. Collins is gone from her room."

Niall was stunned. "What happened?"

"Flemming was standing outside the door when Romanoff, her relief, arrived. He insisted on checking before taking over, but the door was jammed again. They broke open the door. The window was open, and Ms. Collins and her clothes were gone. Flemming checked outside. She said there's a roof outside the window and a fire escape at the other end of the building. We assume she left that way – or someone took her – but it seems more likely that she left on her own. The room was neat as a pin and her gown was folded on the bed."

"It gets better and better, doesn't it? I should have put Flemming in her room. Now we have three possible victims running around the streets. I can already hear the Chief screaming."

"We'll find them sooner or later, sir."

"I hope it's sooner. What did you read about Zaskar, India?"

"Sapphires, sir. I checked on the Internet when Ms. Tadmore told us about the gems from India because I wanted to know what ones would be worth smuggling. Zaskar sapphires were one of the gems I found. The mines were closed around 1975 and they are thought not to exist anymore."

"Very good. If I don't watch out, you'll be taking my job. You told everyone to keep an eye out for Sara Collins as well as our Anne?"

"Our Anne, sir?"

"Yes, Sergeant!"

"Yes, sir, I put the word out."

Niall smiled to himself, grateful that Mettler always knew when to keep his mouth shut.

"Good. Tell Flemming – or Romanoff or whoever is there – to go and sit in Maxwell Good's room. I don't want him to disappear too. I saw Herzog a few minutes ago. Send him to look around Sara's room, and have her window checked for fingerprints. If she was taken, there might be prints – who knows, we might get lucky. Then come back here, and don't mention to the good doctor in there that we don't know where either of the women are."

"Right, I'll just be a minute, sir."

Niall thought about Anne again. She did indeed resemble Maggie, but looking like Maggie was not being Maggie. Maggie was sensible but Anne was trouble. He didn't understand what drove her to keep running away. He'd ask, if they found her alive.

Niall checked his watch and sighed. He was tired and fed up with the situation. It was after ten, and Prabdha apparently had a long slow story to tell. He wished he'd asked Mettler to bring back something to drink. He pushed open the door and walked back into his office.

"Sorry for the interruption, Doctor. If you don't mind, I'd like to wait until the Sergeant returns before you begin your story."

"As you wish, Lieutenant. I hope the news was not anything disastrous. The Sergeant looked troubled."

"No, no, just some bureaucratic difficulties."

"I was reading the poem on the wall. It is quite nice. Did you write it?"

Niall glanced at the framed poem. "No, it was written by my father."

"Ah, you honor your father by keeping his poem on the wall. He must be proud of you."

"He was killed when I was a boy," Niall confessed, surprising himself.

"Ah, then we have a level of understanding." Prabdha looked sad. "If only my son had your respect, this entire situation might not have occurred. It is very painful to me." Prabdha dropped his chin, instantly looking older, grayer, and smaller.

Mettler knocked on the door and entered.

Niall saw that Prabdha was still lost in his misery but said, "Let's begin."

"Yes, you are right. We must begin." Prabdha took a breath that seemed to re-inflate him to his previous stature. "As I was saying, I come from Padum. It is a difficult place but my family was blessed. One day, when my father was a young boy, wandering in one of the passes…"

Prabdha halted and studied Niall and Mettler suspiciously. Niall could see he was making a decision about them before he continued. "He found a distinct stone. He brought the stone back to show his father, who recognized it as a sapphire. My grandfather took his son back to the spot where he had found the stone. When they searched the area, they uncovered several more."

"Our family prospered and as a result, I was able to earn an education. I was the first in my family to attend university. I do not know if you realize what a miracle it was in my country at that time, where almost half of the population was illiterate, to move up in life?"

"I've never been there, but I can imagine," Niall said.

"My grandfather and father were so proud of me. I, in turn, was proud of my son, who received his university education in England, but now I regret sending him."

Niall saw rage simmering beneath the surface. Prabdha's speech became more difficult to understand as he became more emotional, and Niall strained to decipher some of the words. He gathered that something about them finding and keeping the stones was illegal and thought that it was that fear and anger that motivated Prabdha. Niall didn't like the combination, and wondered how to handle the situation.

"Underneath all of those blessings and happiness was the political situation in Kashmir," Prabdha continued.

His love for each of the people he spoke about was clear but Niall also noted the guarded way he had referred to the location of the gems. The man was halfway around the world, and he still couldn't relax; the family secret was safe with him. Prabdha explained the history of the region and Niall let him ramble. The similarities between Indian and Irish history under the English came as no surprise: England had begrudgingly granted each country freedom; religious troubles had followed and continued to plague the surrounding countries.

"My son saw a changed country when he returned from living abroad. His education had changed him as well, and he came home with ideas about freedom for all people, but what he found was a land declining under the weight of Indian rule. He became more and more involved in the convoluted freedom movement. Somewhere along the line, he met a man who claimed to be a freedom fighter, but I have since learned that the man was nothing more than a criminal. Even with all of his education, my son lacked worldly experience and judgment. The fire of freedom burning in him was his undoing, I tell you." Prabdha spoke rapidly now and waved his hands in the air. "He was seduced by the high-sounding political rhetoric and personal charisma of the man. He joined the man's group."

The Homoeopath fell silent for a moment, anger burning visibly on his face. He looked tortured and indecisive, then slowly regained his composure.

"Now we come to the most difficult part. On the one hand, it is necessary for me to tell you, and yet the telling brings me shame. I must also admit my guilt in this affair."

"In our experience people are harder on themselves than others would be," Mettler said.

"Thank you, Sergeant. That is very kind of you. When my grandfather started collecting and selling the sapphires, he also placed some away without telling anyone." He looked at Niall. "You understand."

"Yes, perfectly." They'd held gems back from the government. People withheld taxes all over the world. Niall didn't care how many illegal stashes the family still had in India, but he did care about the ones here.

Prabdha seemed a bit more relaxed or perhaps resigned. "You probably do not know that the Zaskar sapphires are relatively rare. They are a beautiful cornflower blue, slightly milky, and usually run from about 1 to 4 carats in size. The stockpile was as guarded a secret, as was where my family found the stones. There were many rumors in the town about a hidden treasure, but my father always told me it was untrue, and I trusted him. In truth, he had continued what my grandfather had started: They hid a small fortune of beautiful stones for future generations, but told no one. Eventually, my grandfather died. As my father grew older, he was filled with worry about being the only one who knew the location of the stones, so fifteen years ago, he took me to see them. He died two years later. I carried the secret as I waited for my son to mature so I could pass it on to him. It has been a terrible burden for me." He stopped again. The weight of the secret returned to his face and drained the color from it.

"Would you like something to drink?" Niall asked.

"No, thank you. I've almost come to the end of the story. When my son Chandi returned from university, I felt he was ready to learn of the stones. I should have waited. I knew he was involved with those… those terrorists, those murderers, but I did not believe he would betray his family. I realized as soon as I showed him the hiding place that I had made a mistake. The look on his face when he saw the glistening stones told me."

"Excuse me, Doctor, but how much are the stones worth?"

"Well, it depends on market fluctuations, and the quality of each stone, but there were 650 stones with a total weight of 3000 carats."

"And how much is that in dollars?" Niall asked.

"About three million dollars, sir," Mettler responded. "They're worth about a thousand dollars a carat."

"Yes, that is a fair estimate in today's market," Prabdha agreed. "Even though it may seem like a great deal of money, it took my grandfather, my father, and myself eighty years to collect the stones, one by one, little by little. It was the culmination of three generations' work, so I do not think it is so much money."

He looked at Niall as if for some kind of verification, but he remained unmoved by Prabdha's justifications.

"My grandfather insisted we put some aside so our family would not suffer any economic shortcomings again. I have never known the poverty of my grandfather, and he did not want any of his descendants to suffer unnecessarily but my son saw the stones more universally. He said they could help all of our people find freedom from oppression. Two days after I showed him the sapphires' hiding place, he tried to persuade me to donate them to the cause of freedom. I had no reason to doubt his sincerity, but his zeal filled me with fear. I knew he might do something foolish. I decided to move the stones, but I was too late. By the time I reached the hiding spot, they were gone. I was furious and frightened. The stones upon which our future lives depended were gone. I knew the truth, but denied it, and attempted to console myself that perhaps someone had followed us or stumbled on the hiding place by accident. I would have been happy if strangers had found them.

"When I returned home I found the note my son had left in his room for me. All doubt was gone."

The doctor reached inside his jacket pocket, and pulled out a small envelope. He unfolded the single sheet of paper and read it to them.

"Father, by now you will have realized the stones are gone. I am sure you are angry with me, but you must understand how they will help liberate our people. Soon I will return, and you will see that wealth is fleeting, but liberty lasts forever. I hope you can find it in your heart to forgive me."

Prabdha threw his hands up in resignation. "I searched for him, but he was gone. This letter is all I have of him. We never saw him alive again. A few days later soldiers came to my door and told me they had found his body. They said it looked like he had been killed by dacoit, robbers, but I knew the truth. His alleged friends had killed him. I set out to find them.

"That was three months ago. I hired the best men to find the thieving murderers of my son. I have spent much of the family's money in an effort to bring these men to justice. They are responsible for many deaths, and more unhappiness than can be measured. They care only for themselves! They are a plague on the world! They are evil!"

"Calm down, Doctor. Are you thinking of doing something foolish?" asked Niall.

"No, I don't want revenge, I want justice. He was wrong in what he did, but he believed in it, and they stole his life. What good is liberty without chapattis to feed your children? I could not face my other children, if I did not fight to bring honor back to their dead brother and their future. I have another son who is younger than Chandi but more responsible. He is in charge now that I am gone."

Was this man planning to die or was it just a turn of phrase? Niall said, "I'm sorry for your loss, and now we know that the sapphires are the cause of both our problems, but you haven't told us what you know about Sara Collins and Anne Tadmore."

"Yes, the blessed stones of Vishnu are what this is all about. It took the men I hired to find those responsible for my son's death two months, but they found them. The investigators were former Indian military investigators, and they themselves verged on being outside the law, but they were honorable. Two of them were killed in New Delhi, but the third one was able to infiltrate the group. He was the one who informed me about the possible danger to the young women."

"Is he still undercover in the group?"

"I am afraid he, too, is now dead. I believe you knew him as Jimmy Ramdas, but his real name was Satchang."

"They found out he was a plant and killed him," Mettler said to Niall.

"A plant?" Prabdha asked, confused.

"A spy."

"Yes. Perhaps they left him in the house as a message to me, a warning about what might happen to anyone else I sent after them. I should have told the young woman about the danger when I spoke to her the other night, but at that time I did not know they had discovered poor Satchang. It was clear they were in the way – or at least, Miss Tadmore was in the way, as she would not leave Charon alone. She was like a madwoman."

"You have my condolences on the loss of your son," Niall said. "What he did was wrong, but you were wrong, too. In order to avoid paying taxes you lost a son and three people who worked for you. A resident of this town is dead and another is in the hospital. I have two missing women, attempts to kidnap residents off the street, and a group of murderers running around town shooting people. Who knows how many other peoples' lives have been affected because of a handful of stones."

"You are a hard man, Lieutenant, but you are correct."

"Doctor, I'm not sure what you wanted or expected from me, but I can tell you that, if we recover the sapphires, they'll probably be turned over to your government. That is completely out of my hands. What I do need is for you to tell me everything your men found out about this gang. If you don't tell me everything, I'll arrest you for withholding evidence. If someone else dies, and I find you withheld information that would have prevented that death, I'll arrest you as an accessory to the murder. Do you understand?"

Prabdha took a deep breath, then said resolutely, "Yes, completely."

Niall turned to Mettler. "Would you bring us something to drink?"

"Yes sir, I'm sure I can find a cup of tea somewhere."

The two men sat silently during Mettler's absence. He returned after five minutes with a tray in his hands.

"This will make you feel better." He placed a cup of steaming tea in front of Prabdha. Then he deposited the tray with two other cups on Niall's desk.

"Did your man know how they were smuggling the gems into the country?" Niall asked.

"No, he was not able to get that far into their confidence. However, I do know the stones arrived last week, and that Martin Charon was involved with their entrance into America.

"Our final conversation was last Wednesday, five days ago. Satchang told me they were all excited about the delivery of the last shipment that would make them rich. Satchang was going to find out who had the stones and call me back on Thursday. When I did not hear from him, I said to myself that he must be in trouble, so I decided to come here myself. That is also why I telephoned Miss Tadmore and Miss Collins. Since they were connected with Mr. Charon, I feared they might be in danger. Even though I had never met them, I did not want them to end up like my son. As soon as I stepped off the airplane I telephoned the two women, but it was too late for me to stop the tragedies."

Prabdha alternately sipped and blew on his tea.

Niall remembered his mother saying, "A long thread: a lazy tailor." He didn't want to be a lazy tailor. All the threads of this episode had to be pulled tight. He felt as if he might finally be making some headway and would be able to sew it up very soon.

"Did he tell you who is in charge or the names of the people who were all excited about the stones? Did he tell you where they're staying?"

"Satchang said a man named Billy Ananda was in charge, but he had the impression Billy might be taking orders from someone else. I know of three others in this country who are involved. Satchang told me that two were recent immigrants just grasping for a piece of your American dream, but the other is possibly a bad man. I have their names here, along with their addresses," he said, handing the paper to Niall.

One address was in Manhattan; the other two were local. "It appears they aren't as harmless as Ramdas thought – otherwise, he would still be alive, isn't that right?" Niall said, handing the paper to Mettler.

The doctor lowered his head. "It is greed that closes our eyes to right and wrong." He sat silently meditating on his cup of tea.

Niall asked Mettler to run a check on the names and addresses, particularly with Immigration, and to check the name Billy Ananda on NCIC as well, then he turned his attention back to Prabdha.

The Indian said, "Billy Ananda is an elusive man, but I know he was in this area last Wednesday. If he didn't find the sapphires, I am sure he is still near here. He is a very greedy man and would never leave without the gems."

"Did your man find out if Billy Ananda is his real name?"

"He said nothing about it."

"You said your goal was justice. What did you hope to achieve when you found the men who killed your son?"

"I had not completely decided what I would do, although I must admit I considered killing them and taking back the gems.

My father and grandfather misjudged the value of money in the scheme of life. I understand what they were thinking, but they never considered the ramifications. The truth is we only have one thing that saves and bestows immortality upon us: our sons. Shakespeare knew the value of sons; he wrote in his sonnets about the importance of continuing one's line. Do you have children?"

"No," Niall replied. The subject of children stirred up too many unpleasant feelings. Maggie and he had spoken often of having children, but all their plans were destroyed by her illness. "You aren't thinking of leaving town, are you?"

"No, I am here for the destruction of these men. I will be here until that is somehow accomplished or they leave. I would also very much like to claim the body of Satchang and return it to India for a proper burial."

"We may need to keep the body until the case is closed. Come by tomorrow afternoon; by then, I can find out what you will have to do. Are you still staying at the Long Arms Motel?"

"Yes, I will be there."

"Here's my card."

Niall watched the doctor drive away, wondering if he'd made another mistake by letting him go.

* * *

CHAPTER XIII

Niall sat up, gasping for air, and swallowed several times to force back the familiar bitter taste. He slowed his breathing and oriented himself. His phone was ringing, but he ignored it. He hadn't had the dream about his father in almost a year. Reliving his father's death the other night probably brought it on. When he was younger, the dream had kept him awake many nights. If Niall could just finish writing the aisling, maybe the dream would finally disappear forever.

He took a few more slow breaths, then picked up the receiver on the fifth ring.

"Sorry to bother you, sir."

"What time is it, Anthony?"

"A few minutes after six."

"What happened?"

"They found Anne Tadmore shortly after one o'clock this morning, and she's in the hospital. She's not hurt, but she's in shock. One of the three boys who rescued her was killed."

"*Is mor an trua,*" Niall said.

"Excuse me, sir?"

"It means it's a pity. What the hell is wrong with her?"

"I don't know, sir, but the night duty commander put an officer with her. I don't think she'll be running off again – the doctor sedated her."

"How did you find out about all this?" Niall asked.

"Before I left, I asked Herzog to call me if anything happened. They received a shots-fired call around one AM. The address was –"

"135 Maple Drive, right?"

"You've got it, sir. Anyway, a unit responding to the call saw a Jeep roll into some parked cars. When they approached the vehicle, they found Ms. Tadmore in the passenger seat crying and cradling a young man. Tommy Cordero had been shot once in the left side of his head with a small-caliber bullet through the plastic side window."

Niall swung his feet over the side of the bed. Anne Tadmore's name might sound like the words for good luck in Irish but she sure wasn't to those around her, he thought.

Mettler said, "Ms. Tadmore was pretty incoherent, but he must have driven at least a block before he collapsed, though it was amazing he was able to get even that far; he was pronounced at the scene. The Chief is going to call you again. I figured I'd let you know so you wouldn't be completely in the dark."

"Thanks. Did they find the other two young men?" he asked standing and walking to the closet to grab some clothes.

"No sir. Herzog went to Tadmore's house, and found her keys still in the back door lock. The garbage cans were overturned. Forensics is checking out the car and the house. I'm guessing Tadmore and the three young men were looking for the jewels. The jeep is registered to a Peter Drago at an address just three blocks from where Ms. Tadmore's altercation took place last night. Neither he nor Cordero have records. We're still working on the third one."

Niall went to the kitchen and

"Put Drago's name out to the patrol units and have an unmarked one sent to his house. I want detectives sent to the two addresses Prabdha gave us here in town. See if we can get search warrants for the gems at those houses. If they find the men, bring them in for questioning. Send a car over to the Long Arms motel, and bring the doctor back to the station too; I don't want him vanishing when he hears the news. We'll also need to contact NYPD and ask them to check the address in Manhattan – Forty-Seventh Street wasn't it?"

"Yes sir, I think it might be a jewelry store."

"That's exactly what I was thinking. If it is, they're probably using it to sell the gems. We're going to have to call in the FBI, Customs, the State Department, the IRS and who-knows-what other federal agency. I'll let you know after I speak with the Chief. I'll be at the office as soon as I can."

The dream about his father clung to him like the icicle outside his office window clung to the stone. It haunted him and mingled with the murders, the gems, and Anne. The aisling poem wouldn't leave him alone and neither would the memories of Maggie and his father. Niall remembered his uncle teaching him about aislings. A common theme in the vision poem was the fairy woman seeking salvation; the poet always followed the woman. However, Niall didn't feel much like a poet or a savior. Anne was a maid in peril, and she'd been leading him on a wild chase.

But what was really eating away at his peace of mind was that the events of the last two days didn't make sense. The inconsistencies in the case kept gnawing at him. He felt the images way back in his consciousness forcing their way toward the light. He knew that eventually whatever was trying to work its way out would break free. Until then all he could do was stay aware of what was going on inside him. If he tried too hard to figure out what was bothering him, it would only slip farther out of his grasp.

He parked and went to his office where a bottle of water and an apple were on his desk.

Niall had just finished peeling the apple when Mettler walked in.

"Morning, sir. I have some reports from the last few days that you might find interesting."

"Then in truth it would be a good morning." Niall cut a slice of apple.

"What kind of reports have you got?"

"Ballistics from the shooting at 135 Maple, and also the bullet from your car. I have fingerprint results from the same address, and the green Honda. We have a matching set of unidentified prints in the car and the house. The lab is 90% sure the bullets match too – the slug in your car was pretty banged up but they were the same caliber."

"What about the bullet that killed the kid?"

"They're working on it, but it might be a while."

"Get yourself a cup of tea. We'll go over everything we have. The Chief wants it all on his desk before he calls the FBI. If we don't get some results by this afternoon, we might have to take a back seat to the feds."

"Right, sir"

Mettler hurried off in his usual efficient manner.

Questions flew through Niall's mind as he munched on the cool crisp apple: Where were Sara and Charon hiding? Were they both involved? If not, why did Sara Collins leave?

Mettler returned with a cup of tea and another folder in his hand.

"More news, both good and bad; the bad news is that Doctor Prabdha is gone; the good news is that we picked up one of the two men; he's downstairs. His name is Manu Kumar."

"O.K. Let Kumar stew in the interrogation room for a half-hour. Tell me about Prabdha."

"I sent a unit to the motel to pick him up, the manager said he hadn't seen him since he checked in. The paper seal was still on the toilet, and the bed hadn't been slept in. He'd left nothing in the room. We have unmarked units waiting at the motel and at Secaucus Avenue for the other man, Praful Badami, in case either of them return. We're stretched pretty thin."

"Keep people at the hospital watching Maxwell Good and Anne. I don't want them left alone."

They spent the next twenty minutes analyzing and speculating about the degree of each person's involvement. Was Sara really a victim or had she and Anne staged the whole thing? Were Gennifer Bidon and Maxwell Good participants in the crimes or were they collateral victims? Were any of them to be trusted?

Niall said, "It doesn't make much sense, does it? Maybe, Billy Ananda is trying to get rid of Anne – or maybe it's Dr. Prabdha; We haven't verified his story yet. Maybe it's someone else. Perhaps it has nothing to do with the sapphires; it could be a disgruntled customer seeking revenge for paint spilled on a carpet."

"People have killed for less, sir." Mettler lifted his cup to take a sip but it was empty.

"You're absolutely correct. Did the doctor at the hospital say when we'd be able to speak with Anne?"

"Anytime after ten this morning."

Niall glanced at the icicle just in time to see it crack in two; the bottom piece fell to the ground.

"The same person must have killed Joe Madera, Ramdas, and probably even the boy last night, but why? What if we have two separate cases here? Two unrelated incidents makes more sense than a group of gem smugglers running around killing people. Three million dollars is a lot of money, but why call so much attention to yourself? A successful smuggling operation demands a certain amount of secrecy and discretion."

"So why is Charon after Anne Tadmore, sir?"

"She must have something he wants or knows something about the sapphires. He doesn't want to kill her. He wants whatever it is she has, but she doesn't know she has it. We're looking for two different people or groups of people," Niall said.

The phone rang, and Niall answered it.

"It's the call from New York," he said, handing Mettler the receiver. He swiveled his chair to look at the window while he listened to Anthony's one-sided conversation.

"Matt! How are you? Glad to hear it. She's good too. Do you know a jeweler on Forty-Seventh Street named Sardar Pant? That's great."

Mettler wrote furiously in his notebook, as he listened. After he hung up, he said, "They've had suspicions about Sardar Pant for several years, but they've never been able to pin anything on him. Matt said they'd really love to catch the guy red-handed, so they'll keep an eye on him and email us what they've got."

Niall smiled. "The threads are slowly being pulled tighter. We should have a well made suit in no time at this rate."

"You're talking about the lazy tailor again, aren't you, sir?"

They spent the next ten minutes discussing everything from Sara's cold hospital bed sheets to the possibility that Charon was shacked up at the hotel with Gennifer Bidon.

"Sir, you forgot that Miss Collins left her room or was kidnapped during that time."

"Yes, that's right." His forehead had tightened from all the thinking. Niall relaxed his face and shoulders. "I'm sure I'll know more after I speak with Anne. I may even know who is behind the killings. Is the autopsy report finished on Joe Madera?"

* * *

CHAPTER XIV

Niall read the information they'd gathered as he walked toward the interrogation room. Manu Kumar was 27 with black hair and brown eyes. Only 5' 4" he lived by the university where he was a Ph.D. candidate studying computer science. He'd been in the United States five years; his visa was current, and he taught basic computer programming at the university.

"He doesn't seem like much of a criminal, does he?" Mettler observed.

"Not particularly, but he's involved somehow, unless Prabdha was just picking Indian names out of the phone book."

"Anything is possible, but the name in Manhattan makes it unlikely."

As Niall opened the door, he whispered to Mettler, "It's time to play hardball."

Manu Kumar was disheveled. A young, dark-skinned man with a mustache, he sat behind the table, nervously twisting a handkerchief in his hands. A patrolman stood silently in the corner.

"Good morning, Mr. Kumar. I'm Lieutenant O'Huiggin and this is Sergeant Mettler. Sorry we had to drag you out of bed so early in the morning. How are you?"

"I did nothing. Why have you brought me here? I am an Indian citizen. I am…"

"Calm down, Mr. Kumar. Have you been read your rights?"

"Yes."

"If you'd like to have an attorney present, you may."

"I have done nothing for which I need a lawyer."

Niall sat opposite Kumar and said, "Very good. We'd like to ask you a few questions, and if everything checks out, you'll be free to leave. We're hoping you'll be able to help us solve a series of terrible murders. You might know something helpful – even if you're not aware you know it," Niall added, cutting off a protest. Niall smiled while he spoke.

"Of course, if I can help, I would be glad to be of assistance. However, I do not see how I can shed light on the unfortunate murders that have been in the newspapers the last few days."

"Thank you. How long have you been in the United States, Mr. Kumar?"

"Five years, three months and ten days."

"How have your studies been going? Do you like it here?"

"Yes, it is meeting up to my expectations," Kumar said, his face relaxing.

"We'll try and be as brief as possible so you can continue with your day. Where do you come from in India?"

"I was born in New Delhi. My family is well-respected. My father is a powerful businessman," he said with pride.

"Have you ever been to Kashmir?"

"Not for many years. My father owned a small summerhouse there, but it is unfortunately a troubled part of our country. There are terrorists and soldiers everywhere."

"I've heard about the troubles. Do you know Professor Charon at the university?"

His face tightened. "I have had the pleasure of meeting him." Kumar quickly added. "But only through the international students club. He is well-respected by the students and faculty."

A bead of perspiration appeared on Kumar's upper lip. He dabbed at it with his handkerchief.

"Are you aware of his other businesses?" Niall asked, leaning back and crossing his legs.

Kumar blinked. "I am not sure what businesses you are referring to."

"How much longer do you have until finish your degree?" Niall switched directions to keep Kumar off-guard.

"I will be finished at the end of May," answered, growing uncertain.

"What are your plans after you graduate? Would you like to stay in this country, or are you going to return to India?"

"I have been offered a very good position with a company in California. Silicon Valley." Kumar relaxed and his face glowed with pride.

"So you came to America to earn a college degree, then you're off to sunny California to work in a fine company who will supply you with a resident's visa, and you'll live happily ever after. Does that sound right?"

Kumar squirmed. "I am not sure what you mean."

"Did I tell you I'm a painter?" Niall made his slight Irish accent more pronounced.

Kumar looked perplexed. "No."

"I am. I paint pictures of people's futures. Let me paint you an alternate version of your future: I see you not telling me the entire truth this morning. Later, I find out that you withheld evidence that you're involved with the three murders. Do you know what happens? No job in Silicon Valley, no advanced degree in computer science, and your visa is revoked, but as a consolation prize, you find yourself in an American jail for a minimum of ten years. If you live through that experience, you'll be promptly deported to India as soon as they open the steel doors. How's that sound to you as an alternate future? Do you think I'm a good painter?"

A tinge of red suffused Kumar's face, either anger or fear. Undoubtedly, the man was intelligent. He must have had to work hard to reach this point in his education. At times, he also must have been under great pressure, but in all likelihood, he didn't have much experience with this kind of pressure.

"I have nothing to do with your murders. I have done nothing!"

"Where were you last Wednesday night around 7:30?"

"Wednesday? I was probably at home. Why? What does it matter where I was?" Kumar's voice rose a bit. Niall thought he might be starting to panic.

"Were you alone, or were you with Praful Badami?"

"I do not know any such person."

"I guess we'll have to ask your neighbors if they saw or heard you last Wednesday night. We'll ask Mr. Badami the same questions. We'll ask Sara Collins if you were one of the men who raped her, tied her up, and left her to die in a closet. They thought she was unconscious the entire time, but she wasn't. She got a good look at the men, and you fit the description of one of them very well. When she confirms that you were the one who attacked her they'll charge you with rape, attempted murder, false imprisonment and several other crimes."

"That is absolutely ridiculous. She was not raped."

Kumar could hardly keep himself in the chair. His body seemed to have a mind of its own. He moved up and down, back and forth.

"How do you know she wasn't raped if you weren't there?"

Kumar hesitated for a second. "The newspaper said nothing about her being raped."

"We don't allow everything to be printed. I forgot to paint the entire picture of your life, Mr. Kumar, so let me add the few remaining details: You're deported from this country with only the clothes on your back and whatever you have saved from making license plates in prison; you'll be quite a bit older. As soon you land in India, you'll be charged with the murders of young Mr. Chandi Prabdha and at least two other gentlemen. Of course, that doesn't include charges for smuggling, etcetera." He stopped to let the picture settle into Kumar's mind. "Now, where were you last Wednesday night, and what do you know about the missing Zaskar sapphires?"

Kumar sank down in the chair. "I was at Professor Charon's house."

"Thank you. Tell us what happened while you were there."

"We never touched the woman. We only went to tell the Professor that we no longer wanted to be involved in the smuggling. Neither of us wanted to risk our future. I had just learned that very afternoon that the company definitely wanted to hire me; they offered me a very good package. Why would I tie her up or rape her? Why would I jeopardize what I have been working for, for so long?"

Niall and Mettler remained silent but Kumar continued without prompting, spilling everything.

"We were arguing with the Professor, but he told us to be quiet and then went to see if she could hear us. When he pushed the door open, she fell and hit her head on the table. She was unconscious but breathing regularly, so all three of us carried her into his bedroom and placed her on the bed. Praful put a wet towel on her head to bring her around, but she remained unconscious. We gave the Professor back the $3,000 he had given us to help, and then we left. We did not see the Professor or the woman again. I was deeply shocked when I saw the news on Saturday morning. That's all I know – I never even knew her name until then."

"What about Sunday night? Why did you, Charon, and Badami attempt to kidnap Anne Tadmore?"

"Oh, my life is ruined!" Kumar covered his face with his handkerchief and wept. "The shame, how will I ever be able to face my family again?"

"Calm down, Mr. Kumar. If what you say is true, you're not in as much trouble as you could be, and if you continue to cooperate with us, you may come out of this without too much difficulty."

Niall knew Kumar would probably be charged with some crime, but that was up to the DA. He couldn't say whether the university would give him a degree, or if the California company would still want to hire him, or if the feds would allow him to stay. The situation made him sad.

Kumar wiped his eyes. "I will do whatever you want."

"Thank you. Tell us what happened on Sunday evening."

Kumar's voice was subdued. "I was at home. I had not left the house except to buy the newspaper and groceries. I was terrified when I heard what happened to the woman, Miss Collins. Then I heard the news that Ramdas was found dead at the women's house and about the explosion that killed that friend of theirs – I thought the Professor had gone mad. I expected the police to show up at my door, so when the doorbell rang late Sunday afternoon, I almost died of fright. I did not answer it. A short while later the telephone rang, but I let the machine answer. It was Praful, so I picked up the phone. He told me the Professor wanted our help, and if we did not help him, he would inform the police about our duplicitous behavior. 'It will only take an hour,' Praful told me. All we had to do was retrieve the professor's house keys from that woman. The Professor did not know what had happened to them, but he was sure she must have taken them Friday night. The Professor hid the keys in the backyard for Billy Ananda, who was supposed to retrieve them that very night, but they were not in the place where the Professor kept them."

Niall put the pieces together: Anne was looking for Charon on Friday night. She arrived before Billy Ananda and used the keys he was supposed to take to let herself into the house. Instead of Charon, she had found Sara.

"Why didn't Charon just ask her for them?" Niall said more to himself than to Kumar.

"I do not know. Ask me about computers, I can give you answers, but do not ask me about people. I am a failure."

"Do you know where the sapphires are?" Niall asked him.

"No, all I did was go to the airport for Professor Charon and retrieve tea."

"What about Billy Ananda? Is he is in charge?"

"Billy is very smart. I have known him since we were young boys in New Delhi. He is what you call a hustler who prefers to live outside the normal boundaries of life. I do not know why he chooses to live the way he does. He likes excitement, so it may be as simple as that. I am not sure if it was his idea or the Professor's, but Billy is in charge."

"Do you know where we can find him?"

"No, we do not speak often. He disappears for long periods. I have only seen him four times in the last five years, – of that, I am sure. He called me from New Delhi several weeks ago and asked me to do him a favor for the sake of old times. All I had to do was go see the Professor and say hello. One day, about two weeks ago, while I was walking in the hall, the Professor asked me how I was doing, then he told me about his importing business, and asked me if I wanted to make some extra money helping him. I told him I did not have a car; he said it was not a problem. He introduced me to another student, Praful Badami."

"Does Badami have a brown car?"

"Yes, his car is brown. I only made some deliveries of tea for the Professor, and then we went to the airport to pick up a large shipment of tea. It was not until later that I learned there were gems in that shipment."

"Didn't you think it unusual for the professor to give you $3000 for so little work?"

"He gave us the money afterward and told us it was a bonus for a good job. At first, I was very excited, grateful, then I thought about it and spoke to Praful. He told me about the gems. It was then that I started to realize what Billy and the Professor had done to me."

"Do you have any photos of Billy Ananda?"

"At home in India. They would be over ten years old, but if you want one, I can email my parents to send me one. They should be able to scan it and email it back to us very quickly."

Niall nodded. "That would be a great help. Do you know where we can find either Professor Charon or Mr. Badami now?"

"No, after those thugs attacked us, we drove away. I made them drop me near my home. I have not gone out or heard from either of them since."

"That's it for now, Mr. Kumar. Thank you for your cooperation. We'll have to keep you here until the District Attorney decides what to do with you, but I'll tell her how cooperative you've been, which may help. This officer will take you to a holding cell."

The blood, along with hope, drained from Kumar's face. He looked like he was about to faint. Niall felt bad again, but he was used to the feeling. It was part of his job. The officer escorted Kumar out the door.

"What do you think about his story, Anthony?" Niall asked.

"It sounds probable; all the pieces seem to fit. However, I don't think we should take him up on his offer for the photo; we don't know where the other end of the email would be, and I'm not such an expert that I could figure it out. But if what he said is true, it supports your theory about two separate cases."

"Who would want Anne dead so bad that they would wreak havoc all over town? Charon could have killed her twice, but didn't, and is he the one who tied up Sara? Maybe Sara lied about what happened?" Niall mused.

"Good point, sir. Who would suspect Ms. Collins if Ms. Tadmore was murdered? She was in the hospital during Ramdas's murder and she was sedated."

"If she hired someone to kill Anne, the person somehow stumbles on Jimmy Ramdas, and has no choice but to kill him, too. It would have been the perfect alibi. Who would suspect her?

Both Anne and Sara would have been considered victims of the same mad man."

"Yes, sir, but what's her motive?"

"I don't know. I'm only throwing out possibilities."

"Do you think Ms. Collins knew about the gems?"

Niall sighed. "I don't know the answer to that either. It could just be a convenient coincidence. If she did know, she's pretty slick to use them to cover her trail." Niall stopped and considered what he'd said. "Listen to me. I already have her convicted."

* * *

CHAPTER XV

He arrived at the hospital, sent Flemming on a break, and took a seat in Anne's room.

Niall hoped that she'd verify his theory about there being two cases, and perhaps give him the information he needed to pick up the loose threads, but he had to wait until she returned to the waking world. Anne's face was serene and beautiful. The hunger inside him appeared again as he watched her sleep. It had been a good hunger with Maggie, so he was glad it had returned. Then the muscles tensed around Anne's eyes, forehead and mouth and she ground her teeth. Niall wondered about her dreams.

He took out the notebook with the stanzas he'd written over the last few days; but he couldn't finish yet. They were still chasing the fairy maiden.

His father had tried to explain what made an aisling:

"Niall, my boy, did you ever dream of a beautiful woman, and the dream seemed so real that when you woke, you couldn't tell if the woman had been there or if she was only a dream?"

"No Da, I haven't."

"Ah, well, you're only a boy, aren't you? In a few years, you'll understand what I'm talking about. In the meantime, we'll study some nice aisling poems."

Anne mumbled something unintelligible. He imagined a fairy creature who looked like her, wondering if he were talking himself into a delusional state.

"Would you like me to come back now, sir?" Flemming stood in the now open door.

"No, I'll stay. I need to speak with her as soon as she wakes. Go and give Applebaum a break for a few minutes."

"Well, if you need anything, I'll be out here."

She closed the door, but the latch didn't catch; it drifted open slightly. Niall heard Flemming and Applebaum chatting in the hall, but didn't pay much attention until he heard her mention Joe Madera.

"I couldn't believe he was dead; I had seen him only an hour or so earlier. He visited Sara Collins and then he was dead, just like that." He heard her snap her fingers for effect.

"Makes you think, doesn't it?" Applebaum replied.

Madera had been to the hospital before he died, so he could have told Sara where Anne was staying. Sara could have used the phone to relay the information to her hired killer or she could have talked to the killer on the roof outside her window.

"Who's Maggie?" Anne asked.

Niall felt a stabbing pain in his chest. "Ah, you're awake. How are you feeling?"

"I guess I'm O.K. Who's Maggie? I heard you yell her name in the street last night and almost came back. I wish I had come back." Anne wiped the sleep from her eyes.

"She was my friend. She died several months ago."

"I'm sorry. I know how hard it is. I can't believe Joe and Tommy are dead." She pulled herself to a sitting position. "Do I remind you of her?"

"Sergeant Mettler says you look a great deal like her."

She smiled. "I'm not asking him, I'm asking you. What do you think?"

"You do remind me of her."

"Is that why you look so serious?"

"I always look serious when I'm protecting beautiful women." Anne smiled again.

"I've been lying here hoping last night was all a dream but it wasn't. Tommy is dead."

"I'm afraid he is, but before you get yourself all worked up, I want you to know it wasn't your fault. Do you hear me?"

"Yes. What about Pete and Mike? Are they O.K.?"

"As far as we know. We haven't found them yet. Do you have any idea where they could have gone?"

Anne shook her head. "You have to find them before they're killed, too. They were looking for the tea. Pete thought it was hidden at my house or Martin's office. I should have stopped them from going. Tommy would still be alive if I'd stopped them."

"We'll find them, Anne." Niall thought it was far too late for recriminations. "The last few days have been crazy enough to destroy the strongest person. Just stay calm."

She gave him a doubtful look.

"We have things to talk about. We – you and I – have to stop the person or persons who've killed your friends."

"What can I do?"

"The first thing is please don't run away again."

"I'll try."

"Lovely. Now, tell me what happened after you left the hospital last night," he prompted.

"I ran for a while. Then I remembered about Maxwell's car and thought I'd get it and drive to Manhattan until everything calmed down. I couldn't deal with Joe's death, the guilt, the shame, and the embarrassment. It was stupid to think I would have been able to hide driving a Rolls Royce, but I was confused."

Niall couldn't believe she'd even thought she would be able to take the car.

She continued, "Along the way, I saw Pete, Mike, and Tommy. At first, I thought they were going to harass me, and then after walking a block or so I realized they were following me. I began to panic and walked faster towards the boulevard. I passed through the rundown section of Lowell Woods and was into the yuppie part when Martin popped out from behind a tree. I almost had a heart attack. I couldn't believe he had found me, but he said he had been watching the hospital. He told me he had a car waiting and wanted me to go with him. I told him to forget it, but he grabbed my arm." Anne waved her arms as if fighting Charon.

Niall moved his chair closer to her bed. "It's all right."

She stopped her movements. "I'm fine. It will take more than reciting a story for me to get worked up at this point. Anyway, then a dark car pulled up and two Indian guys jumped out. The three of them were pulling me toward the car when Pete, Tommy, and Mike ran up and starting hitting them. Martin and his Indian friends jumped into the car and took off. Pete told me they saw Martin following me and decided to see if I needed help. They invited me to Pete's sister's house two blocks away. We stayed there for a couple of hours. Marta and her husband were having a small party and when the guests left we slipped out with them. Marta's car was parked in front of the house. I even wore a disguise in case anyone was watching."

"What kind of disguise?" Niall asked.

"I just switched coats with Tommy, and Marta loaned me a hat. I held onto Mike when we went to the car, pretending to be his girlfriend. He got a big thrill out of it." She laughed. "We didn't see anyone around, so we drove to Pete's house, where we switched to his car. He didn't want to take the chance of damaging his sister's car. Ráfe would have gone berserk."

"Who's Ráfe?" Niall asked.

"Marta's husband. She's really sweet but him, ugh, he's a tyrant and an asshole. He gave me a look before we left that made my skin crawl. The oddest part of it was that they were Indian too."

"Who?"

"Ráfe and his relatives. When I first arrived, I thought I had fallen into a trap."

"The world is filled with coincidences but I'll check them out. So you went back to your house and then what?"

Niall looked at her hanging clothes and her bulky parka. He should have checked it while she was sleeping, but it was too late now.

"We drove around the block to make sure there wasn't anyone watching, then found a place to park on Osage Street, behind my house. Pete and Mike went to my house to search for the tea. I waited in the car with Tommy."

A tint of red highlighted her pale cheeks. "They wouldn't let me go with them in case Martin had gone there. I gave them my keys so they could look around inside. Pete thought Martin might have hidden the tea in the garbage cans. He told Tommy if anything went wrong we should meet them at the secret place or something like that."

"Do you still have the keys to Martin's house?"

"I threw them away. They came out of my pocket when I gave Pete my keys and I tossed them out the car door because I was still pissed at Martin."

Niall's stomach tightened. She had to tell those kids about the gems. Now one was dead. Then she threw the keys away. He had the urge to wring her beautiful neck.

"We have information that one of those keys is the key to where the sapphires are hidden," he told her, watching her face carefully.

"Sapphires?"

He thought the surprise on her face was genuine, but wasn't certain. "Yes, they are what you were looking for. We've uncovered some interesting facts since you took off last night. By the way, your garbage cans were searched on Saturday morning, and there wasn't any tea, used or otherwise."

She looked thoughtful. "I remember an odd key on the ring. I tried it in his door on Friday night but when it didn't fit, I used the other one."

"Excuse me while I call Sgt. Mettler and send some people out to see if they can find the keys."

"I'm going to freshen up." She was more alert than a few minutes ago.

Anne shuffled into the bathroom and closed the door as he dialed.

"How are things going?" he asked, Anthony.

"I'll be done within the hour, sir."

"Excellent. It seems Anne threw Charon's keys away on Osage Street, where she parked a few doors from the house directly behind her house and they should be in the street near there. It's still early so maybe we'll get lucky. If they can't find them, have men canvas the houses to see if any of the neighbors found the keys or saw anything."

"Yes, sir. How's she doing?"

"I think she'll be fine when this is over. By the way, the first name of the third young man is Mike. Has anything else come in since I left?"

"Only that there isn't any record of the mysterious set of fingerprints."

Anne came out of the bathroom and crossed the room to the bed. Her cheeks glowed and her green eyes blazed. Niall thought about how fresh Maggie looked in the morning. It had been one of the joys of his life to see her, but now she was gone. Anne was not Maggie and could never replace her.

He told Mettler, "I'll be finished here soon. Meet me at Peter Drago's house. Drago's sister, Marta, is married to an Indian guy named Ráfe. They live on Sussex, two blocks down from Mrs. O'Halloran. Find out what you can on him."

Back in bed, Anne propped the pillows behind her head and pulled the covers up to her waist. Except for the glimpse of her bare shoulder the other night, this was the most he'd seen of her; the other times she'd always had her parka pulled tight around her.

"Do you have any enemies?" he asked.

"Enemies?"

"Yes. Is there anyone whom you've offended so badly that they might want to kill you?"

"I don't think so."

"When, precisely, did you exchange coats with Tommy?"

"Pete and Mike had just left the jeep. I was freezing, and Tommy wouldn't turn the heat on, so I asked him for my coat back. I stuck Marta's hat on his head." Anne started putting the pieces together. "You mean it was me they were trying to kill? They thought Tommy was me."

"I'm sorry, Anne, but it appears that way from the information we've been gathering. Someone might be using the gems as a cover to kill you."

"But why? I mean, who would want to kill me?"

"Can you think of anyone – a former boyfriend, a customer that was especially unhappy with your work – who holds a grudge against you? How do you and Sara get along?"

"You're not suggesting that Sara would want to kill me!" Anne pulled the covers up to her neck.

"What do you think? Is she jealous of you? Did her relationship with her father change after you started living with them?"

"I was only five years old – and Sara was only four. Besides, Sara's been in the hospital since Friday night, and she was locked in the closet for two days before that. How could you think she would do such a thing?"

Niall sat at the foot of the bed in hopes of calming her. "I'm only asking what you think."

"You're making a mistake. Bring Sara here, and I'll prove it to you."

"Do you remember early last night when you came to see her? We went into her room. The door had been blocked, and the sheets were cold, but she told us she'd been sleeping."

"Just bring her in here, and I'll show you you're wrong," Anne repeated.

"I can't. She vanished an hour or two after you ran out of the hospital. There were no signs of a struggle in her room. Her nightclothes were folded neatly and left on the bed."

"I don't understand. Sara's the closest thing I have to a sister. We've shared almost everything all our lives. We took care of her father together when he was dying."

Niall had long ago lost count of victims who'd been killed by loved ones – spouses, siblings, children and parents. They only hurt the ones they love.

"Is there someone else who might be angry enough with you to try and kill you? If Sara's not involved then she may also be in trouble and need our help."

"Y'know, I don't have that much of a life; I work most of the time. The only person I can think of who might have had wanted me dead for some reason would have been Joe." She shrugged. "As far as clients go, I've had good relations with all of them, and so has Sara."

"You can't think of anyone from your past who might still be angry enough to come after you?"

"No, no one. Until last week, I lived a quiet life. I haven't even left town in a month."

"Tell me about Sara. You must know everything there is to know about her."

"I thought I did, until the other day."

"Has she had many boyfriends?"

Anne relaxed her grip on the covers and they dropped to her waist. "She had a steady boyfriend for two years, David Montaigne. I thought they were going to get married, but then he started acting strange. It was weird."

"What did he do?"

"He bought her really cheap and hokey gifts. Sounds petty, doesn't it? But it was bizarre. One night he wanted to go to a party, but Sara didn't want to go. They argued for a long time.

She finally gave in. When they arrived, she discovered it was BYOB and there was an entry fee. David wouldn't even pay for her. She gave in then too – to avoid a scene, but left almost immediately. After a big fight the next day, she dumped him."

"Did he bother Sara after they split up?"

Anne waved a hand dismissively as she said, "He called a few times trying to work things out, but it was too late as far as Sara was concerned. Men never know when the relationship is going downhill. Women start distancing themselves and working out their feelings long before men do."

"I'll keep that in mind. When did they break up?"

"A year ago, I think it was March – Oh! I know. It was a Saint Patrick's Day party at some bar in Manhattan."

"So Sara never saw him again?"

"We bump into him sometimes. In fact, we saw him right after Thanksgiving. Sara and I were out with two guys from the paint store. I only went because she thought one of them was cute," Anne said, qualifying the experience. "They turned out to be real turkeys. I think they spent too much time breathing paint fumes. That was the night we ran into David."

"How did he act when you saw him?" Niall asked.

"He pretty much just said hello and walked away. His date was giving him dirty looks so he didn't stand around chatting," Anne laughed. "Sara's date that night turned into a real pain in the butt. He called her all the time, trying to make another date, but she blew him off. We even stopped buying paint in that store, and made a pact not to mix business with pleasure again."

"What were their names?"

"Sammy was the one Sara dated. He wasn't around long enough for me to learn his last name. Dennis Travis is the other. They both worked at Mel's House of Color on Hohokus Boulevard. Do you really believe Sara could be responsible for Joe and Tommy's deaths?"

"I don't know who's responsible, but we're well on our way to finding out. I hope for your sake it isn't her." He stood and pushed the chair back against the wall. "Remember, Anne – stay here! I don't want you to get hurt."

* * *

CHAPTER XVI

Lunch was being delivered to patients as Niall left the second floor. He toyed with the idea of stopping for a tuna fish sandwich but realized he was eager to see what happened at Mel's House of Color. He checked a phone book for the exact address. The sky was dark and a mass of gloomy clouds spanned the horizon. The thirty-degree temperature felt almost balmy after the bitter cold of the last several days. He inhaled the familiar odor of snow; but snow wasn't the only scent – the smell of his quarry seemed stronger. He was finally on the right track.

Niall assembled a mental checklist as he drove with all the players and assessed them for possible danger – either to themselves or to others. The gems were a real problem and if too many people found out about them, they might end up like Tommy Cordero.

Martin Charon was probably a threat only to himself. He was too smart for his own good, and it would only be a matter of time before he came out of hiding.

Niall didn't see Maxwell Good as a problem. He had just stumbled into the mess while repaying an expensive debt.

Dr. Prabdha, on the other hand, was a wild card who could cause trouble. The man was too emotional and might snap if he were cornered. Prabdha had told him that Billy Ananda was dangerous. Manu Kumar's story, and the story Anne related to him about Martin's experiences, backed up the doctor's story. But, he still didn't know if Billy Ananda was even in the country.

What about Sara? Niall had spoken to her twice and didn't have a sense that she was dangerous. What had Joe Madera said about her? Ah! That she was 'so kind and lovable'. She had probably either been kidnapped or was a pawn in someone else's game. But whose?

Madera had been a lost soul; Niall had felt it from their first meeting. The autopsy would take place soon; Niall would attend in hopes of finding out exactly what had happened at Good's studio. Too bad Madera had died, though, as Niall would have liked to have pinned all the trouble on him.

He saw a gaudy sign for Mel's House of Colour and wondered if there really was a Mel as he parked in front of the store. He stayed in the car to watch, attempting to pick out Sammy and Dennis Travis in the small group behind the counter, then went into the store.

The smell of paint was strong and reminded him of Good's studio. A man wearing white paint-speckled painter's pants waited for his order to be filled, while a smartly dressed young woman bantered with one of the three sales clerks behind the long counter. The salesman was in his late twenties and wore a wedding ring. The second sales clerk was a short, balding man. He looked flustered as he bustled around at the back door checking a shipment that had just been delivered. The third sales clerk efficiently added measured quantities of color into the open cans of white base, then sealed and attached them to the mixer. He was tall, about twenty-five years old, and had long blond hair.

Niall knew the tall blond man had to be either Sammy or Dennis Travis. He wished he'd gotten a description of the men from Anne. The other two didn't fit his image of the kind of men Sara would date, but who knew.

Niall wandered around the store while waiting his turn. The woman and the painter paid their bills and left.

"Do you need any help?" asked the lanky blond worker.

Niall flashed his identification. "I'd like to speak with Dennis Travis, and another worker named Sammy."

"I'm Dennis. Sammy is not here. What's the problem?" The young man looked like he'd been expecting him.

Two new customers came in, and the short, balding man watched them from the back of the store.

"Can you step outside for a minute?" Niall asked Travis.

He sighed and yelled to the back of the store. "Mel, I gotta take a break for a couple of minutes."

"Who's going to help the customers?"

"It's not my idea." He motioned at Niall.

Mel made a face, dropped his clipboard on the pile of boxes, then trudged to the front counter.

When they reached the street Niall asked Travis, "Where were you last night around one AM?"

"Home in bed. I don't usually go out on Sunday nights because I have to be here at seven every Monday. Does this have something to do with Anne and Sara?"

"What makes you think that?" Niall asked moving to the curb.

"I've been reading about them in the paper for the last few days, so I had a hunch you guys might come around asking questions. I'll tell you before we go any further that I haven't seen either of them in two months."

"Tell me about your relationship with Sara Collins and Anne Tadmore," Niall said.

"I just told you that I don't have a relationship with either of them. I only went on the date with them because Sara wouldn't go without Anne, and Sammy kept bugging me to go." He kicked at a piece of paper.

"You didn't have a good time?"

"Don't get me wrong. Anne and Sara are babes, but I only went because Sammy wouldn't leave me alone." He smiled and added, "If I'd have scored with Anne, I would have been happy, but it didn't really matter because I've got a fine old lady. Do you understand what I'm saying?"

Niall felt a twinge of anger listening to Travis talk that way about Anne and decided to push him a little, even though he knew it was childish.

"Yes, I understand. Did it upset you that they stopped buying paint here and wouldn't go out with you again?"

"How many times have I got to tell you that I didn't care? I only went to shut up Sammy."

"Tell me what happened on this date."

Travis kicked at another piece of paper and sighed. "Sammy makes a great first impression, but after ten minutes of listening to him, most people realize he's a zero. Sara and Anne knew it within five minutes. I could tell Sara had decided to drop him when the date had barely begun. The rest of the evening was totally uncomfortable for everyone – except Sammy. I've never met anyone as thick as him. He's stupid, but thinks he's a world-class brain."

"What do you mean?"

"Sammy thought we were both gonna score; he had no idea what was going on. I think it's because he's slow and so wrapped up in himself. After dinner, the dude wanted to take the girls somewhere for a drink, but Anne said she wanted to go home. I could tell Sammy was pissed, but he maintained his cool to impress Sara. He tried to kiss Sara when she was getting out of the car, and she blew him off. That's when I found out that Sammy doesn't take rejection very well. He thinks so much of himself that he had his own name tattooed on his back. Shit! He really lost it after we drove away. He was banging the steering wheel and screaming like a lunatic. I thought he was going to have an accident. He made me nervous."

"Was that the last time you saw Anne or Sara?"

"No. They came in and bought paint several times. I was friendly with them, but I noticed they stayed clear of Sammy. About two weeks after the date, Anne told me Sammy had been calling Sara, and his calls were starting to scare them. Anne said she might have to talk to Mel about it, but I asked her to wait a day or two; I told her I'd talk to Sammy and see what he had to say."

Travis looked in the store. Mel was signaling for him to return to work.

"Just another minute and we'll be done," Nïall said. "So what did Sammy say when you spoke to him?"

"I didn't. The store was really busy that day, and he left early for some appointment. By the next day, I'd forgotten. I don't think Anne and Sara came in again."

He wouldn't meet Niall's gaze, so Niall guessed Travis had purposely avoided talking to Sammy.

"How did your boss react when they stopped buying paint here?"

"Mel didn't know they decided to go somewhere else until three weeks ago, after several women complained about Sammy's behavior and threatened to take their business elsewhere. It didn't take Mel long to put two and two together. I heard him calling some of the regular women customers he hadn't seen in a while. He heard what they had to say and flipped. Mel apologized to the women, and promised it would never happen again. He even told them he'd give them an additional ten percent discount for a year. Later, I heard him talking to his lawyer on the phone; he was afraid he'd end up being sued."

"What did he say to Sammy?" Niall asked.

"He went berserk. I never saw Mel like that before. It was wild. Yeah, it was really wild." He drifted off for a second, then he said, "Mel's smart. He waited until the end of the day, then called us all together. I think he wanted to impress on us what would happen if we screwed around with his customers. He yelled at Sammy in front of us for ten minutes, then fired him, and paid him in cash so he wouldn't have to see him again."

"And that was about three weeks ago?"

"Yeah. The day after Christmas."

"Did you see or speak to Sammy after he was fired?"

"He was really depressed, and asked me to go with him for a beer as soon as we walked out the door. I didn't want to go, but he begged me. I never saw him drunk before that night. I tried to leave several times, but he kept buying me beers. He's a bad drunk and by the time he dropped the last of his pay on the bar, he was in a foul mood. He had convinced himself that being fired was Anne and Sara's fault."

Dennis Travis stopped and Niall could see he'd realized the implications.

Travis added, "I don't think he meant to do them any harm, though; it was just drunk talk. You know how it is when you get a few beers in you."

"What's Sammy's last name and address?"

"Sloan, Sammy Sloan, but I don't know where he lives."

"Have you seen him since the night he was fired?"

"Nope – and I don't mind telling you I'm happy he's gone. There's less tension in the store now. I didn't realize it when he was here, but he had weird energy." Travis searched Niall's face and said, "You think it is Sammy who's doing the killings, don't you?

"At the moment, I don't have a suspect," Niall said, but he was smiling inside. Sammy's actions placed a lot of the picture into focus for him. He thought Sammy looked good for the killings, and he might even have been responsible for Sara's closet experience.

Mel came outside. "Dennis, can't you see the store is full of customers? What the hell do you think I'm paying you for? Are you trying to shorten my life?"

"Mel, this guy's a cop and he's asking me about Sammy. What do want me to do?"

"Do I look like a schmuck? Of course, he's a cop. Now get inside, and take care of the customers. I fired Sloan for trying to ruin my business and I can find someone else to do your job, too."

Mel held open the door for Travis, then started to follow him inside.

Niall stopped him. "Excuse me, Mel, I'd like to ask you a few questions."

"I don't have time. I'm trying to run a business here."

"It will only take a few minutes, or we can go to the station. It's your choice."

"Come inside if you want to talk to me. I'm not standing out here freezing my tokhes off while you ask me about that schlimazel."

Niall followed Mel into the store, past the counter, and into the back. Mel went straight to his office, pulled out a file, and tossed it on his crowded desk.

"There it is. That's all I know about the good-for-nothing putz."

Mel sat down, and pulled his chair close to the desk. The room was cluttered with papers. Niall didn't see a computer in the room. Mel was old school: He had everything in his head. If something happened to him, it would take ages for anyone to figure out his system.

Niall looked through the file. Mel kept all the time cards. He'd also made notes on Sammy's character and behavior.

"How long has it been since you last saw Mr. Sloan?"

"It's all in there. I made a record of it, just like my lawyer said. What more do you want?"

"Aren't you the least bit interested why I'm looking for him?" Niall asked, irritated by Mel's attitude.

"I've got a business to run. He doesn't work here anymore, and I'm not interested."

Niall didn't like Mel's stick-your-head-in-the-ground outlook on life, and was about to say something, but Mel was one step ahead of him.

"I know you're thinking I'm a hard ass; I can see it in your eyes. You probably even have me labeled as a tightwad Jew, but I tried being nice to them and nearly got screwed. The business is going down the tubes because of the chain store competition. My wife has ovarian cancer, and my son is in his last year of medical school. I'm in debt up to the rafters and holding on by a slim thread. Do you blame me for acting this way when I discover my trusted employees are driving away the customers?"

"Why don't we start over again? I'm Lieutenant Niall O'Huiginn, Hilltop PD."

Niall held out his hand to Mel, who eyed him for a second and then relaxed. He shook Niall's hand.

"I'm Mel Nebeling. What can I do for you, Lieutenant?"

"I'm sorry to hear about your wife, Mr. Nebeling, and I wouldn't trouble you except we have a murderer running around town."

"Do you think it's that good-for-nothing, Sammy?"

"At the moment, I'm trying to gather as much information as I can about him. There is the possibility that he is in some way connected, but I'm not sure."

"I know all of them," Mel sighed.

"All of whom, Mr. Nebeling?"

"Anne, Sara, Sammy, Maxwell Good, Martin Charon, and Joe Madera." He held up his hands and counted off the names one-by-one on his fingers.

Niall raised an eyebrow, but otherwise kept his face impassive and his tone casual.

"How do you know Charon and Madera?"

"The town isn't that big. Charon comes here to buy small cans of paint for his house. He's always touching up something. I think he's got some kind of aversion to dirt. And Madera used to come here sometimes with Anne, but I haven't seen him in ages."

"I see Sammy's address here. I don't suppose you have a picture of him?"

"I don't."

"Can you describe him?"

"He's a few inches shorter than you and has brown hair and brown eyes. Now that I think about it, he looked kind of like Joe Madera, except his hair was shorter."

"Thank you for your help, Mr. Nebeling. I'm sorry to have taken your time, and I hope everything turns out well for you."

"You don't by any chance need some paint, do you, Lieutenant?"

"Not at the moment, but I'll keep you in mind when I decide to paint."

"We give personal service, and I'll give you a ten percent discount."

"I'll remember that, thanks."

The apartment house on Laurel Place was an older, brick-faced, four-story building, relatively well kept. Niall studied the buzzers. Sammy Sloan's name was listed for 3B.

A short, grizzled man left the building with an armful of boxes.

"Whatch you doing here?" he demanded in a thick Spanish accent.

"Who are you?" Niall responded.

"I'm the superintendent. If you have no business here, then get lost. I have enough headaches without perverts hanging around the front of the building. Go on, beat it."

O'Huiginn flashed his badge. "What's your name?" he asked.

"Armando De Leon," he said grudgingly.

The super rolled his r so his name sounded like Arrrmando. He walked around the bottom steps and headed toward another set of stairs leading to the basement. Niall followed and De Leon continued his voyage under the stoop.

"I'd like to ask you some questions about one of your tenants."

De Leon searched his massive key ring for the one that would unlock the padlock.

"He's not here. I haven't seen him in almost two weeks."

"We are talking about Sammy Sloan, aren't we?" Niall asked, astonished that everyone knew who he was looking for, and yet not one of them had bothered to call with information.

"There's no one else in this building that would bring the police here."

DeLeon found the correct key and opened the door. He lifted the boxes again, and walked into the gloomy basement. Niall followed him warily, but the super stopped a few feet inside, and went through the same procedure with his keys to unlock another door.

"Do you have a key to Sloan's apartment? I'd like to look around inside it," Niall said.

"There's not much to see. I took everything that was any good."

"He's only been gone two weeks, so why are you cleaning out his apartment?"

"He hasn't paid rent in five months. The owner has been trying to get him out of there. Sloan's gone so that's that. We're selling what stuff we can to get back some of the money. The landlord told me I could keep thirty percent of what I recover. I need it to pay off the Christmas bills. I'm poorer now than when I lived in Puerto Rico."

"Do those boxes contain some of his belongings?"

De Leon looked directly at Niall for the first time.

"Why you gotta come here and cause trouble?"

"You and the landlord are the ones who are going to be in trouble if you don't answer my questions."

"O.K., O.K., it's his stuff, but it's not worth much. I already throw away most his other junk. I have to clean the place and paint before I can rent it again."

"You're going to have to take all of his belongings back upstairs and leave them there – and untouched – until I tell you otherwise. Is that clear?"

"Why you bother honest people? How come you didn't come throw that bum out when he wouldn't pay the rent?"

"You have to follow the law, Mr. De Leon. Tell the landlord what I said. I'll let you know when you can finish cleaning the apartment. In the meantime, let's go upstairs and see what's left."

The unhappy superintendent put the lock back on the door, and picked up the boxes. Niall walked outside and waited for him.

"Don't you need some kind of warrant to search his place?" De Leon asked as he ambled up the front steps, obviously in no hurry to please Niall.

"I'm not searching it, Mr. De Leon. I'm only having a look around. It will take only a few minutes, and then you can get back to work. I'll send over some men with a search warrant in a few hours. I hope you will cooperate with them."

"Sure, I cooperate. I told him not to rent the apartment to Sloan, but would he listen to me? I know trouble when I see it coming."

They climbed to the third-floor landing while De Leon mumbled the entire way.

"Hold these."

The super handed the boxes to Niall. They were heavier than they looked. Niall was impressed with the man's stamina. The superintendent pulled out his set of keys again and immediately picked out the apartment key to 3B. He unlocked the door, pushed it open, and went inside.

"Drop the boxes wherever you want," De Leon said over his shoulder.

There wasn't much in the bare studio apartment. A lone wooden chair sat in front of an old Formica-covered metal table. The windows were bare and sparkling clean. A stained mattress leaned against the wall next to a stack of six boxes.

"You did a good job of cleaning."

"I ain't got no time to waste. The landlord pays me to take care of the place, and that's what I do."

Niall checked the kitchen cabinets, but they had all been emptied. The bathroom was also spotless.

"Did you find anything unusual while you were cleaning?"

"Unusual? What unusual? The place was filled with junk. Look at that crappy mattress. The studio was filled with that kind of filth. All I did was move the garbage out into the street where it belonged."

Armando De Leon stood in the doorway with one arm stretched out against the doorframe. He tapped his foot impatiently while Niall opened one of the boxes he'd carried into the apartment. It contained a video camera and a few dozen videocassettes.

"You didn't find any weapons or any bullets while you were cleaning, did you?"

"No, nothing like that. He had piles of dirty magazines and empty beer cans. I saved his clothes for him in case he came back, that's the kind of guy I am. They are downstairs in boxes. I hold no grudges against the son of a bitch even though he spits at me when I ask him for the rent. The son of a bitch spits at me, and I save his clothes for him. What kind of man does that make me?"

Niall said, "Calm down. I don't think you'll have to be worrying much about Sloan from here on out."

Niall went through the contents of the boxes, but didn't find anything that struck him as a connection between Sloan and the incidents of the last few days.

"That's all for now. The other officers should be here within an hour or two. It won't take long for them to go over the apartment and if you're cooperative, they'll be out of your way much sooner."

"Sure I'll cooperate. I cooperated with you, didn't I?"

Niall pushed another box of junk aside. "Yes, you did."

De Leon took a cigarette from a pack in his shirt pocket and put it between his lips. He searched his pants pockets for a match but couldn't find one.

Niall lifted the last box and pulled it open as the super went to the kitchen, opened a drawer, took out a book of matches, and lit his cigarette. He walked over to where Niall was wading through a collection of old rock and roll records.

"Here, you didn't check these. Maybe there's some evidence in here." De Leon flipped the book of matches into the box. They fell between well-worn copies of The Beatles', *Sergeant Pepper's Lonely Hearts Club Band* and the *White Album*.

The surly building superintendent annoyed Niall, but he kept himself under control. He was looking for a picture of Sloan when he saw the book of matches at the bottom of the box. They were from Sammie's Restaurant and Bar, the same as the book of matches he'd seen at Anne's house on Saturday morning. It was a small connection, but it was all he needed to convince himself. He scooped them up and slipped them into his pocket not wanting to give the super the satisfaction of knowing he'd inadvertently helped him

"Did you find any pictures of Sloan when you were cleaning?"

"I found porn pictures only. I burned them all." When Niall gave him a stern look, he said, "Not many personal items in here, not pictures, not letters, nothing. He had a stack of unpaid bills but I burned them too. Screw him and the other people he didn't pay. He spits on me when I ask for the rent. Pheww, I spit on him and his family."

Niall had enough. "That's it for now. Thank you for your cooperation. Here's my card; if you remember anything that might help, call me."

De Leon looked it over thoughtfully. "What did he do that they send a lieutenant looking for him?"

"He killed two people who kept asking him for money," Niall lied. It was a terrible thing to do, but he couldn't control himself. As far as he knew, Sloan's biggest crime was skipping out on his rent. However, the last three people he'd spoken with had upset Niall and this was his little revenge.

De Leon's antagonistic demeanor wavered. "You bullshitting me, right?"

"Listen to the news, Mr. De Leon. Listen to the news."

Niall walked out of the apartment and waited at the head of the stairs. The super followed him out and locked the door. The cigarette dangled from the corner of his lip. The smoke snaked its way up De Leon's face and into his right eye. He locked the door and dropped the heavy key ring back into his pants pocket without taking his eyes off Niall.

He squinted at him through the smoke and said, "You bullshitting me, aren't you? You just janking my chain. I know you cops."

"I bet you do. I'm trusting you to stay out of there until the officers arrive. I hope you've been honest with me. There's a lot at stake here, and I'd hate to have to come back to arrest you."

"I told you everything. Do I look like the kind of man who would lie?"

"If I find out you didn't tell me everything, I'll be back."

As Niall started his car, De Leon stood on the front stoop watching him, still trying to figure out if Niall had been yanking his chain. Niall smiled at him as he drove by the building.

The man smiled back, wagged his finger at him, and yelled, 'I know you screwing with me. What kind of man you think I am?'

After Niall arranged for forensics to process Sloan's apartment, he called Mettler.

"How's everything going over there, Anthony?"

"I've been trying to reach you. How come you turned your phone off?"

"I didn't feel like being interrupted while I was thinking. Is there a problem?"

"No, sir, it's just that you're out there by yourself and could get into trouble."

"That's very kind of you to be so concerned, but I'm a big boy. Did you finish the report?"

"Yes, sir. I was about to give it to the Chief. Do you want to hear what I found out about Ráfe and his wife?"

"You can tell me at Peter Drago's. I'll be there in a few minutes, and I'll wait out front for you. If the Chief asks, you haven't heard from me."

"Yes, sir, I'll be there in no time."

Niall parked at Peter Drago's house, put a tape of Céilí music into the player, and contentedly let his mind wander.

He'd been there fifteen minutes when a large snowflake landed on the windshield and melted; he watched the remnants trickle down the glass. He opened the window, looked up at the gray sky, and sniffed at the air.

"Smelling for the bad guys, sir?" Mettler asked as he walked up to the car.

"It smells like snow. Get in and we'll have a chat."

Mettler walked around to the passenger side and eased his large frame into the seat.

"Would you like something to drink, sir? I have herb tea, warm chicken soup, and fresh carrot juice."

Mettler took three containers from a brown paper bag and placed them in a row on the dashboard.

"You're a regular delicatessen. I'll take the carrot juice. I could use an energy boost. How's everything back at the station? Did you give the Chief the report?"

"Yes sir, he wants you to call him on a land line." Mettler handed him the cardboard container and then looked indecisively down at his knees.

"What is it?"

"He figured you wouldn't call. So he told me to tell you that the budget is, in his words, 'really shot to hell.' If you don't resolve the case by this afternoon, he's turning it all over to the FBI. They didn't find the keys, either. They're canvassing the houses now, but it doesn't look good."

Niall sipped carrot juice as another snowflake splattered onto the windshield.

"It's not a blizzard, but something is changing, Anthony. Maybe one of the neighborhood kids found the keys – or someone on their way to work. Don't look so down. We'll think of something. In fact, I'm beginning to get an idea on how we can bring everyone together. I don't care that much about the gems, but I do want to catch the killer."

"I don't like to have a case taken away from me, especially when we're making headway," Mettler grumbled.

"Hah! And you're the one telling me I'm too involved."

"It's professional pride, not personal involvement," Mettler replied.

"I know, I know, but we're not in New York. This is a smaller department. We can't spend an entire year's budget on one case. Tell me what you found out about the other people."

"Ráfe Alunzi is Peter Drago's brother-in-law. He's been in the US for seventeen years. He married Marta Drago two years ago; he's twelve years her senior. He imports carpets from India, has a shop in downtown Manhattan, and he has a clean record. That's all I could find on him. The other thing is that Tommy Cordero's father has been down at the station for the last hour and a half demanding to know what we're doing about his son's murder."

"Someone went to see the boy's parents last night, didn't they?"

"Yes sir, Herzog went, but Mr. Cordero is not the kind of guy who's going to sit home and wait for us to call. Anyway, I calmed him down. He told me the third boy's last name is Rodriguez. The three young men were always together. None of them has a record, but the local patrol unit knows them. The officer told me they were relatively good kids who could have gone either way.

They've been questioned a few times after burglaries, but there was never any proof they were involved. The boys don't have any gang affiliations and pretty much keep to themselves."

Niall told Mettler what Anne had told him and then filled him in on his visits with Mel and the superintendent.

"Sounds like Sammy Sloan deserves further scrutiny, sir."

"I agree. I told the super not to touch the apartment again until we check the place. He either confiscated or discarded all of Sloan's belongings. Forensics should be on their way over there now, so it won't be long before we know if our mysterious fingerprints belong to Mr. Sloan."

"Very good, sir. You're beginning to sound like a real detective."

"Why thank you. I'm working on it."

Mettler took a sip of the herb tea. "By the way, the Rodriguez family lives in the same building as Peter Drago and his family."

"Let's go see if either family knows where their little boys are hiding. You ask the questions. If I need to throw in my two cents, I will."

"Yes sir." Mettler placed the white plastic top back on his container of tea.

Fifteen minutes later, they were back in the street, none the wiser for their interviews.

"I know what to do Anthony. It's risky, but I don't see any other way. Let's go to the hospital to speak with Anne because it won't work without her help. Then I want you to go to the office, find out what you can on David Montaigne and Sloan, and see if your friend in Manhattan has anything on Ráfe and his carpet shop. While you're there, tell the Chief he can give it all to the FBI right now if he wants."

"Is that your plan? I thought we were going to see it through to the end," Mettler protested.

"This is part of my plan. The sapphires are a dead end – we're not going to catch the killer chasing after them, so let the FBI spend their budget on them. We have to concentrate on Anne. We've allowed ourselves to be confused by the issue, and it's worked in the killer's favor. I have a feeling the killer is, as my mother says, an amadan."

"A what, sir?"

"It's Irish for a fool. If I'm right, he's going to try again, and we're going to give him the opportunity to do it. That's why I'm going to talk to Anne. In order for my plan to work, she'll to have to cooperate. I thought about just putting her out on the street, but there's no telling what she might do. Also, if anything happened to her because I… Well, let's say the consequences would be very unpleasant."

"I guess they would, sir. We're taking an awful chance, aren't we?"

"Not 'we', Anthony – me. If anything goes wrong, you were just following my orders. You have a wife, a mortgage, you're trying to have a kid, and I don't want to put any of that in jeopardy. I don't have much choice. I either surrender the case to the FBI or I do what I have to do."

* * *

CHAPTER XVII

The snow was falling steadily by the time they reached the hospital. Flemming was leaning against the wall outside Anne's room reading a book as Niall and Mettler stepped from the elevator. She closed the book and put it in her pocket.

"She's still in there, isn't she, Flemming?" Niall asked.

"Yes, sir. She's been sleeping on and off. I just stepped out here for a change of scenery."

"Be of good cheer; you're almost done with this assignment. I'm going to talk to her, and I'll fill you in afterwards." Niall turned to Mettler. "Anthony, get the ball rolling. Call Herzog, Phillips, and Carmody."

As Mettler walked away, Flemming asked, "Can I ask what's going on, sir?"

"It might be better for your career if you don't know what's happening."

He opened the door to Anne's room. She was asleep. The room smelled slightly sweet and the fragrance sent a rush up his spine. Her face was peaceful, almost angelic. Niall wanted to wait until she woke by herself, but it was almost two in the afternoon and time was important to his plan.

"Hi, Niall." Her voice was soft, filled with sleep. "I hoped one of these times Flemming would be gone. It's nice to see you." She smiled at him.

Niall smiled back, "Did the doctors give you more sleeping pills?" He wanted to make certain she was in a state to understand him.

"No, I'm just catching up on my rest. There didn't really seem to be any reason for me to stay awake. If you stay, I promise not to go to sleep again."

He felt himself pulled toward her. He remembered Maggie saying almost the same thing. The emotion was intoxicating. Niall turned away from Anne to break the spell, got the chair and dragged it closer to the bed.

"I came to have a serious talk with you," he said, sitting.

"I don't want to hear it if anyone else is dead." She put her hands over her ears. "I also don't want to hear it if you still think Sara was involved in the killing. I can't believe she would ever want me dead. What would her motive be? It wouldn't be the business because Sara doesn't care much about it. Her father left her enough money to live comfortably for the rest of her life. The house is the only thing that we both own, and I don't care that much about it. Besides, we've lived together, worked together, and seen each other every day for the last twenty-four years. We haven't been separated for more than a week at a time since my parents' death. Sara has never shown any signs of violence or hate toward me or anyone else. There's no way she would want me dead, and that's that."

Niall let her get it all out of her system. She may have been drifting in and out of sleep, but her mind hadn't been snoozing.

There was a knock on the door and Flemming stuck her head in. "Maxwell wants to know if you feel up to a visit." She sounded cheerful. Flemming had become chummy with Maxwell and, it seemed, with Anne, too.

"Yes, I'd love to see him," Anne replied brightly. Her mood had changed three times since she started speaking.

"Not right now. Tell him later," Niall said.

The door closed. Anne looked disappointed.

"I didn't give you a chance to tell me why you came, did I?" she said.

"First, I'm glad to see you're feeling better. Second, I want to ask you to help me catch Tommy's and Joe's murderer." He scooted his chair closer to her. "I have to warn you that there might be some danger, but it's the only way I see to stop them from killing again. I'm taking every precaution to protect you. I don't believe that Sara is involved, but she's probably in a dangerous position at the moment, and you might be helping to save her, too. It's probable that the longer you stay here, the more dangerous it will be for her."

He stopped to evaluate the effects. Anne was probably more than content to lie in bed and let the rest of the world go its merry way, yet, she probably also felt she owed a debt to Tommy, Madera, Maxwell Good, and Sara. The more Niall stared at her, the more he wasn't sure if he was doing the right thing, but Anne had to make the decision.

"If I can help, I want to help. Tell me what to do."

"Go home and wait."

Anne's face grew dark.

"You're using me as bait?"

"Don't worry. I'll have detectives in the houses surrounding yours. Sergeant Mettler contacted the owners, and men are being sent at intervals to wait for you. Everything should be set to go within an hour or so. I'm going to slip into your house before you arrive, and I'll wait with you as long as it takes."

"We'll be alone in the house?"

"No, not entirely alone; there'll be a listening device so the other detectives can hear what's happening inside at all times." Niall studied her face and decided to give her another option. "If you prefer, Sergeant Mettler can wait with you."

"I think you'll do just fine, but your plan sounds an awful lot like a TV show."

Niall grinned. "It was the best I could come up with under the circumstances. Let's hope the perpetrators don't watch as much TV as you do. If you'll get dressed, I'll go take care of the paperwork, and in an hour you'll be on your way."

"So that's the entire plan? I go home and wait for the person to come and kill me?"

"Four detectives will be watching your house, and I'll be right there with you." Niall smiled at her as a further reassurance, but he was worried. "You'll be fine. I'll see you at the house."

"Has it started snowing?"

"About an hour ago, and if it keeps up we might see a good amount on the ground by tomorrow." His voice trailed off as he remembered the poem, the murderer, and his resurfaced desire. Which one was the most important?

"What? Why are you looking at me like that again? Are you taking one last look at the condemned before she's led off to the slaughter?"

"No, that's not it at all. I was thinking of a poem. I'll send your friend Flemming back to keep you company."

"Wait a second. How can you make a comment like that and then walk out of the room?"

"I was only kidding about Flemming." It was a weak and obvious attempt to cover his slip. He felt his face redden.

"Not that, the thing about the poem. If I'm going to allow myself to be bait, then I want to hear the poem."

"Anne, we haven't got time for that now. I've got work to do, things to arrange, and killers to catch. I promise, I'll give you the entire poem later."

He stepped into the corridor.

Flemming said, "Sir, I've been thinking, and I'd like to be in on whatever you're planning. I know you don't like me, but I wish you'd give me a chance to show you that I can do the job."

"I have nothing against you. You just need more experience."

"How am I supposed to get the experience if you won't give me the chance?"

Niall wasn't sure if he should let her in. She was young and determined to make her mark on the world. He appreciated her spunk, and the experience would definitely be good for her, but if things went wrong, her career might be affected. Mettler and the others were veteran detectives who could handle themselves in any situation. He had enough responsibility with Anne's life weighing on him without worrying how Flemming would act if the situation didn't turn out the way he planned. She also didn't know he hadn't cleared his plan with the Chief.

"I appreciate your willingness to do the job, and I'd like to say yes to you. However, there's something you have to know first, but I'm not going to tell you unless you give me your word that whether you come along or not, you won't reveal to anyone what I'm about to say. Is that clear?"

"Yes, sir. I won't say a word."

"I don't have approval for the actions I'm about to take. The Chief doesn't know and probably would say no. If you come along, you could either get a commendation or be punished if the plan goes awry. Do you understand?"

"Yes, sir, but I still want to help."

"O.K., but you've been warned. Don't fail me, Flemming."

"I won't, sir. What should I do?"

"I want you to wait about a half hour. Then drive her home." He hooked his finger toward Anne's room. "Walk her inside the house like you're checking to make sure everything's fine and then leave her there. Go change into plainclothes, then meet Sergeant Mettler at 138 Maple, it's directly across from their house. Be as inconspicuous as possible when you return. If anyone is watching, I don't want them to suspect anything is happening. The neighborhood must look as normal as possible."

Flemming beamed. "Yes, sir, I've got it. You can count on me."

* * *

CHAPTER XVIII

Niall waited in the shadows of the small room just off the living room. The chair was uncomfortable, and his butt was sore after three hours in it, but that was part of the job. The curtains were drawn and the lights were low.

Anne dozed in the ratty-looking armchair she'd said had belonged to her father. He watched her slow breathing, wanting to reach out and touch her. He'd never had these feelings during a case; they disturbed and confused him. It would be unprofessional to allow himself to become involved with her. Besides, the poem was almost finished, and he didn't want to chance destroying the delicate creative opening that Anne's presence had produced for him. Mettler might have been correct about him being too involved with her; he had been shooting disapproving glances at Niall every so often since Friday night. But Niall's past and Anne's present consumed him and he had to see this through.

His radio earpiece suddenly came alive. He was about to tell Mettler and Herzog that someone was leaning on the switch, but Niall welcomed the distraction, so decided to listen.

Mettler was saying, "How does this sound, Herzog? The shooter arrived late Friday night at her house, but didn't know that Ms. Tadmore had already left because of Mr. Charon. The killer unexpectedly met Ramdas, who was probably looking for the keys too, so the first murder was just because Ramdas was in the wrong place and the killer didn't want anyone to be able to identify him after he finally got to Ms. Tadmore.

"Somehow, he – and I'm assuming it is a he – found out where Ms. Tadmore was staying and planted a bomb, but she was gone again. I don't understand how the shooter knew where she was staying, but either someone told him, or he's smarter than us. We might never have located Ms. Tadmore if the Lieutenant hadn't figured out the connection between the two women and Joe Madera."

"I guess that's why he's the Lieutenant and we're the second string," Herzog replied, sounding uninterested in Mettler's theories.

"Perhaps."

Niall could tell that Mettler didn't like Herzog placing him in an inferior position. The drone of their voices, his sitting in the same position, and the heat had taken their toll. He closed his eyes, but continued to listen.

"Unfortunately for him," Mettler said, undaunted, "Joe Madera blundered onto the scene and was killed instead of Ms. Tadmore. Then Tommy Cordero was shot because the killer didn't know Ms. Tadmore had switched coats with him. The pieces don't fit together as nicely as I'd like. I guess we'll have to see who shows up at this shindig."

"It's really snowing hard. If this keeps up, we won't be able to see past the front fence let alone all the way across the street," Herzog said. "They're not making much noise in the house, are they? Do you think they're getting cozy, Sarge? I wouldn't mind being trapped with her. Play a little-hide-and-seek if you know what I mean."

"Just keep your eyes open, Danny."

"Yeah, but do you think the Lieutenant has a thing for her? I noticed the way he looked at her. What do you say, Sarge? You're as close to him as his own mother."

"I wouldn't know."

Remembering that Carmody, Flemming and Johnston could also hear the conversation, Niall felt a rush of anger but he had enough control of himself to wait until the appropriate moment arrived before he said anything. However, Mettler's diplomatic handling of the situation impressed him. Did Mettler know the radio was on? Could Mettler be so devious? Mettler would make lieutenant, and maybe one day he would be Chief. Niall didn't have that ambition and wondered what it would be like working under Mettler.

"We've been here for three hours," Herzog complained as if he had never been on surveillance.

Mettler replied, "The Lieutenant didn't really expect anything to happen until after dark. Just keep yours eyes and ears open."

"Jeez, the snow is piling up. It'd take us five minutes to get over there if something happens."

"I'm aware of that, but we'll make do."

"I didn't even bring my boots, Sarge. My new shoes are going to get ruined."

"Shut up, Danny. You're getting on my nerves."

"Someone's looking out the window," Herzog said.

Niall realized Herzog must be talking about this house. He opened his eyes and looked at the chair, but it was empty. He jumped to his feet and went to the doorway. He saw that Anne had pulled apart the curtains and was looking out the window.

"Oh, shit," Herzog said. The radio went dead.

Anne looked like an innocent child watching the snow spiral to the ground. Niall felt the desire to reach out to her rising again inside him.

The radio came to life again in his ear. "Sir, can you hear me?" Mettler asked.

"Yes, Sergeant, I heard you both very clearly."

There was a moment of silence and the radio crackled to life again.

"Sir, we can see Ms. Tadmore from here. If we can then someone else might be able to see her too."

"I'll take care of it."

Niall moved quietly toward her. He didn't want to break the spell of the moment, but knew he had to get her away from the window.

"Please don't stand in the window. You're making Sergeant Mettler nervous."

She turned her head and smiled. "Sorry, but it's the first snowfall, and it's beautiful. I couldn't resist sneaking a peek. Look how deep it has gotten since we arrived home. It is so pure and white that I almost believe nothing is wrong. Come here and look." Anne reached out her hand to him.

Niall had felt a dizzying surge of emotion when she'd said 'since we arrived home'. When she extended her hand, inviting him to touch it, he had to take a deep breath to control himself. He ached to hold her hand but didn't dare. Their words were being scrutinized by his subordinates.

"I can't go near the window, and you have to get away from there. You're putting yourself in danger."

Anne dropped her hand, and her smile vanished. "Sorry, but I'm bored."

"Stay away from the window or you may end up dead."

He pulled the curtains closed as Anne returned to her father's armchair.

She said, "You may be used to all this waiting, but it wasn't what I had in mind when I told you I'd help. The sitting around is getting on my nerves. My bedroom's a mess. There's blood on the floor, and I don't know how I'm going to sleep in there again. I also don't feel comfortable without Sara here. There's so much to do, and I can't bring myself do any of it."

"Why don't you light a fire, turn on the television, or go make something to eat?" Niall suggested.

She remained silent and motionless. Her moods changed faster than the crystalline snowflakes falling to the earth. The dim light inside the house lent itself well to his mood. The evening was taking on a surreal atmosphere. He began thinking about the good times with Maggie before she became ill. Sadness rapidly descended on him.

Anne slipped off her chair and prepared to light a fire. She wadded up old newspapers, placed them on the shiny black metal grate, placed some kindling on top, carefully arranged a few small oak logs over the kindling, then wadded more newspapers and finally put some additional kindling on top of the second layer of paper. When she opened the flu with a metallic clank, several wayward snowflakes drifted onto the newspapers and kindling. She lit a match. The burning newspapers sent sparks shooting up the chimney, and the flames added more light to the scene. Anne was kneeling in front of the fireplace, the right side of her face a blaze of dancing red and yellow firelight while the other half remained shaded.

Niall stood in the doorway between the two rooms watching her. Her movements fascinated him.

"It would be better if you turn on a few more lights," he said to ease his tension.

Anne pouted. "I just don't feel like it."

"The house needs to look like you're home. If they don't think anyone is here, they might not bother to come for a visit."

Anne took three catlike steps, reached out, and turned on the lamp next to her father's chair, then she slid backwards to the fireplace and sat cross-legged in front of it.

The radio crackled in his ear, and Mettler said, "It might be a good idea to turn on the lights outside the front and rear doors too, sir. Then we can see if anyone arrives."

Niall stuck out his left hand and flipped the switch next to the door. "Is that better?"

"Yes, sir."

Niall said to Anne, "Would you please go and turn on the backdoor light?"

Anne continued to poke at the fire. Orange and yellow cinders shot up the chimney as if looking for a moment of peace away from her incessant prodding. She reluctantly dropped the poker back into the bronze rack. She stood slowly and turned to him.

"Would you like something to drink while I'm there, Niall?" She started toward the kitchen.

"A glass of cold water would be nice, thank you. And keep away from the windows as much as possible."

The way she acted made it hard for Niall to believe she was almost thirty years old. She seemed unfettered by the events of the last few days while he carried the weight of his life heavily.

"Are you sure you wouldn't like a hot cup of tea? Martin brought us tea whenever he visited. Yes, that's it, I'll make you a cup of tea. I'll check and let you know your choices." She seemed reinvigorated by the idea.

"Water will be fine," he said, but the swinging door had already closed and the light went on in the kitchen.

He walked over to stand silently next to the door. He heard her checking the piece of cardboard on the broken windowpane. A short click told him she had flipped the light to the backyard. She sighed, and then he heard her cross the kitchen and turn on the water. The water was loud, but he could still hear her opening and closing the cabinets. He also felt the vibrations in the wall behind him as she opened and closed the doors. Then Anne uttered a low, startled sound. He almost entered the kitchen but decided against it. It was the only room in the house that didn't have thick drapes. He would have been visible to anyone in the backyard.

"Is everything O.K., Anne?"

"Yes, it was just a small mouse trying to keep warm. It's gone now."

He heard her return to the sink and run water into a teapot. It was a comforting sound that reminded Niall of family. She put the teapot on the stove and the automatic ignition of the gas stove clicked as she filled a glass.

In an instant she had turned off the faucet, the clicking of the stove stopped, and she was standing next to him, her sudden appearance surprising him. She smiled one of her pixy-like smiles and took him by the hand. Niall didn't resist. Anne led him to her father's chair and placed the glass on the table. Then she gently shoved him down.

She put her mouth next to his ear, and whispered, "Every time I look into the cool gray of your eyes, I feel like I'm looking through timeless portals into another world."

She slipped away, leaving Niall stunned. A small bead of sweat emerged on his forehead, as he watched her walk back around the dining room table.

She lifted her bottle of Calvados, and said, "Remember, you give me one of your poems, and I'll let you have a taste of this." She placed the bottle back on the table and strolled through the doors into the kitchen.

Mettler's voice crackling in his ear broke the spell. "Is everything all right, sir? Do you need a break?"

"No, everything's fine. She's in the kitchen making herself a cup of tea," he said into the radio.

He didn't know what Anne was doing, or why she acted that way, but he knew the effect it was having on him. She certainly wasn't acting like a woman who'd lost two men in a week, and whose best friend was missing. Maybe she was in shock. Was it possible that she'd killed them? He'd better distance himself or something bad might happen to him too.

He raised his voice and said, "Don't stay in there too long, Miss Tadmore. We need you in here."

"I'll be right there, Lieutenant O'Huiginn." She sounded irritated.

Niall was certain the detectives couldn't have heard what she'd whispered to him. He wondered if he should have taken Mettler's offer of a break.

Herzog was right about Mettler knowing Niall as well as his mother did. If the shoe were on the other foot, Niall would have ordered Mettler to let someone else wait with her. However, the race had already started, and it was too late to change jockeys. If the murderer saw people walking in and out of the house, they would have wasted their time. Besides, the air in the house was so thick with sexual tension, that he didn't want one of the other detectives picking up on it.

Anne stuck her head into the room. "I decided to make you a cup of tea anyway. I think you'll enjoy this blend. Unfortunately, I don't have any milk to go with it."

"Plain tea is fine." He didn't tell her that he'd never liked tea.

"It will only take another few minutes for the water to boil, and then I'll be back." She closed the door again.

"Stay away from the windows."

"I'll be careful."

Niall decided that sitting in her father's chair next to the fire was too dangerous. He took the glass of water, wiped the water spot off the table, went to the other room, and placed the glass next to his uncomfortable, but safe chair.

"Niall, I have a surprise for you."

"What now?" he mumbled.

The radio squawked to life. "Someone is coming," Mettler said.

"Save your surprise for later, Anne. Forget the tea and get in here. We have company."

She was next to him in a flash, looking nervous and unsure.

Mettler's voice crackled in his ear. "A brown car just pulled up in front of the house, probably the same car Mr. Charon used last night. There are two men in it."

Niall told Anne, "Stay here and don't worry. It might only be your friend Martin and one of his Indian cohorts. They're probably still looking for the keys."

"I don't think so."

Her response caught him by surprise. "What do you mean?"

Mettler's energized voice reverberated in his ear: "Listen everyone! They're out of the car and heading toward the house. I can't quite make out who they are in the dark but be ready."

Niall moved into the shadows of the adjoining room. Anne put her arms around him and squeezed until she was pressed tightly against him. Her fragrance rushed to his head like a direct sugar injection. He barely resisted wrapping his arms around her. Then Anne lifted her head, looked into his eyes, and kissed him. It was a sweet and gentle kiss. His heart was racing, but he couldn't stay in view.

He put one hand on her cheek and said, "I'll be right here. Let them into the house."

"What if they start shooting as soon I open it?"

Her hands shook. It struck him that Anne had never believed anyone would arrive at her door and that's why she'd been playing with him.

"Don't worry, I'll be right here."

"That's easy for you to say; I'm the one they'll be shooting."

The doorbell rang.

She slipped her right hand into the pocket of her bulky gray sweatshirt. The bell rang a second time. She took a deep breath and turned the doorknob.

Niall pulled his automatic from under his jacket. The wind and snow pushed at the door. Anne struggled to keep hold of it.

"Good evening. I am Doctor Ramchander Prabdha. I called several times in the last few days. Are you Miss Tadmore?"

"Yes, Doctor. We spoke late Friday night."

So the Doctor was still looking for the gems.

"May we come in? The snow and cold are blowing into your house."

"Yes, of course. I've been expecting you."

Niall thought Anne was doing well. He knew that as soon as she closed the door Mettler and the rest would take up positions outside the front and back doors. Prabdha pushed the other man into the room on a gust of wind and snow. Anne closed the door behind them and walked to the middle of the room.

"Come over here where it's warm. I just lit a fire."

"That is very kind of you, Miss Tadmore. I am sorry for our sudden visit. I realize you have been through a great deal in the last several days, but I thought you would appreciate meeting one of the two men behind all of your sorrow. I present to you Billy Ananda." He pushed the man further into in the room.

Anne stood with her back to the fireplace. Prabdha and Billy Ananda had their backs to Niall.

"We're on our way, sir," Mettler announced in his ear.

"The three of us are in position outside the back door, Lieutenant," Carmody said.

He clicked the radio button once for O.K. Twice was the signal for them to come into the house.

Billy Ananda's hands were tied behind his back, and the portion of his face that was visible looked pale and drained. Anne gave Ananda the once-over, stopping at his snow-covered cowboy boots.

"You were at Ráfe's house last night, weren't you?"

"Unfortunately, Miss Tadmore, he cannot talk."

"Why not?"

"It is rather unpleasant. You are undoubtedly better off not knowing."

"Then, how do you know it's him?"

"I mingled with my fellow countrymen this morning. They were most helpful. I found his hiding place after visits to only two shops. I went to the address and found him at home. After some persuasion, he told me where the sapphires are hidden, but he is now speechless. I must make sure he told me the truth, and then I will exact payment for the murder of my son."

"He killed your son?"

Her eyes shifted briefly in Niall's direction, and he hoped the doctor didn't pick up on her slip. He hadn't counted on Prabdha being so persistent.

"He killed my poor Chandi in a remote spot in the Zaskar mountain ranges of India. Then he had the temerity to steal our family's sapphires from him."

Anne looked apprehensively at Prabdha's captive. "He doesn't look like he could kill anyone."

Her eyes shot nervously back and forth between Prabdha and Niall. She was losing the battle with her nerves, and he was tempted to put an end to the situation.

"Do not be fooled by his reserved appearance. If the opportunity arose, he would kill both of us." Prabdha prodded Billy Ananda with his left hand.

"He's also not shy about ruining people's lives," said a third male voice.

Niall was shocked by the sudden appearance of this wildcard. Where had he come from? Who was he? He had to decide the best course of action with too little information.

Both Prabdha and the silent Billy turned at the sound of the man's voice.

Anne looked in Niall's direction again, her nervousness turning to fear.

"You are Mr. Charon," Prabdha said, pulling a pistol from his pocket. "Please, move over here where I can see you better."

"What's the gun for?" Anne asked.

Niall knew she'd asked to alert him. He was still trying to figure out how Charon had gotten in the house; his men had been watching the house for hours. He must have been in the kitchen the entire time.

The doctor said, "I meant you no harm, Miss Tadmore. It is these two men who have ruined my life and they have brought me down to their level. They took away everything of value in my life. My son and my family are lost to me. The coming generations will suffer because of these men's greed. They will now pay for the future misery of my descendants. The gun is the means to deliver the justice they merit. I knew Mr. Charon would eventually come to see you, but I did not realize blessings would be bestowed on me so soon. Now, I have the two of them. All that remains is for you to give me the keys to Mr. Charon's house, and we will be on our way."

Niall heard Charon chuckle grimly, and the sound of his footfalls on the carpet, but he still couldn't see him. His best guess was that he had stopped near the dining room table.

Anne hesitated for a second, looked at Charon, Prabdha, and then shot a quick questioning glance in Niall's direction. "Sorry, I threw them away last night."

"I, too, am sorry for that, Miss Tadmore."

The tone of Prabdha's voice sent a shiver up Niall's spine. The doctor no longer cared about himself or anyone else; he only wanted revenge. Niall had been a fool to let him wander around town the other night. He was sure Prabdha intended to kill Anne as well.

"Maybe we can find them. I threw them in the street around the corner last night," Anne said, pointing toward the back of the house. She was holding her own in spite of her fear.

Niall had one finger on the radio button and one on the trigger of his gun.

"That would be quite impossible in this storm. Several inches of snow have covered the streets. No, I am afraid we will all have to go," Prabdha sighed.

It was the break Niall hoped for. He clicked his radio button once. Mettler would know what he was thinking. All they had to do was walk outside. Niall prayed they'd all go along with Prabdha's orders because there was no way for him to signal Anne without making his presence known.

The doctor began to wave his gun around. "Let us go, Mr. Charon and Miss Tadmore. You won't need coats."

Niall could see the fear in Anne's eyes. Prabdha walked around her and Billy Ananda and stood next to Anne's father's chair, his back to the fireplace. Anne and Billy were between Niall and a clear shot at Prabdha.

"Please, let us not make this any more unpleasant than it already is. Will you all move?" Prabdha pushed Billy Ananda into Anne, knocking her back.

The teakettle whistled. It started low and built quickly into a frenzy. Prabdha looked at the door, puzzled by the unexpected sound. Then he ducked as a bottle struck the fireplace and shattered against the brick. As Prabdha fired a shot at Charon, the Calvados became a blue-flamed inferno as it made contact with the burning logs. Some liquor had also splashed on the carpet and the flames spread rapidly across the floor as Niall raised his weapon and rushed into the room.

The front door flew open, Mettler and Herzog burst into the room with weapons drawn, blocking his way for an instant. Two more shots rang out. Niall pushed past Mettler running toward Anne. She stood rigid with her arms wrapped around herself for protection; her face was blank as she attempted to comprehend the chaos around her. Billy Ananda grabbed at her to hold himself up, and then went down face-first in front of her with blood shooting from his mouth. Anne backpedaled to the front window, and pulled at her sweatshirt pocket as Niall rushed to her.

Carmody, Flemming and Johnston pushed through the kitchen door. The kettle continued to screech in the background as the detectives shouted for everyone to get down. Niall saw Carmody dive in the direction where Charon had gone down.

Prabdha fired twice at Anne; one bullet barely missed her head.

Flemming fired two shots at Prabdha who took cover behind Anne's father's chair as more shots rang out.

The room was filling with smoke as the fire spread. Niall caught a faint whiff of apple mixed with the acrid odor of the burning wool carpet and then the drapes next to the fireplace burst into flames.

He was almost next to Anne when he saw Prabdha's head appear from behind the base of the now-burning recliner. Mettler and the other detectives rushed the flaming chair. Anne leaned against the window, still looking dazed. Prabdha raised his gun and aimed in her direction. His arm was burning but his face was locked in a grotesquely blissful smile as he tightened his finger on the trigger.

Anne screamed, "I didn't do anything," as Prabdha pulled the trigger.

Niall heard a flurry of gunshots ring out, then Prabdha's bullet smacked into the side of his head and sent him into darkness. The force of Niall's body took him and Anne through the closed window. Their combined weight yanked the heavy curtains off the wall and saved them from being cut by the breaking glass. They landed on the snow-covered bushes outside the window and slid to the ground.

Out of the darkness, Niall saw Maggie, wearing the same clothes she'd worn the first time they'd met. Her hair was shiny and her eyes were sparkling green. He'd forgotten how beautiful she had been before the cancer took its toll on her. Her last painful days were the most vivid.

"Hello, young Niall. How are you?" she asked, imitating his mother.

Niall laughed. He always laughed when she said it, but he was confused and his heart was bursting with emotion.

"I'm fine, but I've really missed you."

"You're not fine. Look at you! Why didn't you listen me, Niall? I knew you wouldn't keep your promise and get on with your life."

"I've been trying, Maggie, but life isn't the same without you. How come I haven't dreamt of you before now? Why are you here?"

"I came to make you happy. I came to give you a proper good-bye. Come here and hug me." She opened her arms.

Niall did as he was told. He put his arms around her and buried his face in her hair. It was a familiar smell. He held on tight. He felt safe, warm and cleansed.

In the far-off distance, he began to hear Anne calling him. He didn't want to leave Maggie but the sound of Anne's voice grew louder and louder.

"Niall, are you all right?" Anne kept asking. Her voice, unlike Maggie's, sounded panicked. "Niall! Answer me! Damn you!" He heard her scream. "I can't move. Help me!"

Niall felt large hands lifting him. Anne scurried from under him, and he felt lonely and cold again.

"Are you all right, Ms. Tadmore?" he heard Mettler ask.

"I think so. Is Niall O.K.?"

A crunch of fresh snow echoed in Niall's ears as Mettler knelt next to him. He felt large hands examine his head.

"Looks like the bullet creased his skull. He's semi-conscious. Ambulances and the fire department are on the way."

Niall opened his eyes and saw Anne standing above him, staring at her house. He followed her line of sight. The open space where the window stood a minute ago was a roaring blaze.

"Oh God, look at the house. Can't we put it out?" She ran to the front door.

"Ms. Tadmore, stay away from there," Mettler yelled.

"There's paint and thinner stored in the garage. It might explode if the fire spreads that far, and I have to save the truck."

Niall turned his attention to Herzog, Carmody and Johnston dragging the bodies of Billy Ananda and a smoldering Dr. Prabdha from the house. Charon sat handcuffed and weeping in the snow, wide-eyed Flemming standing guard over him.

Anne ran past them all and through the front door, accompanied only by the crackling explosion of superheated glass. The fire was roaring.

Anne ran out of the house with an armload of books and clothes and dropped the pile in the snow, then she ran to the garage, stuck a key in the lock, and pulled on the handle. The door didn't move.

"Please help me!" she yelled.

Niall tried to rise, but Mettler pushed him back to the ground. "You'd better stay down, sir."

For the first time Niall realized Mettler was holding him.

"Hello, Anthony, I'm glad to see you."

"It's good to see you back too, sir."

"She still needs help, Anthony. It isn't over."

"Yes, sir. Herzog, get over there and help her open the door."

"My pleasure, Sarge." He trotted in his new shoes to the garage door and shook it, trying to free it from the snow.

Anne and Herzog pulled at the door again and again. It came up slowly at first, then opened rapidly when it finally cleared the built-up snow. Anne ran into the smoke-filled garage and Herzog ran in after her. He returned carrying boxes and stacked them away from the house. Anne backed the truck through the deep snow, down the driveway, and into the street. The distant sound of sirens cut through the falling snow. Anne stumbled back across the street. She knelt on the pile she'd pulled from the house, threw off her wet sneakers, slipped on heavy brown boots, and climbed into her big green parka.

Herzog and some of Anne's neighbors carried the last remaining boxes of paint out of the garage. Anne watched them for a second, looked at the burning house, and started back toward Mettler and Niall.

Niall told Mettler, "Keep your eyes on the crowd for familiar faces, Anthony. It's not over yet."

"I will, sir, just rest here until the ambulance arrives. You might have a serious concussion."

"I'm sorry that you're going to have to take the heat, Anthony. Tell the Chief you were just following orders."

"Don't worry, sir. I'll handle it."

Niall felt a warm hand on his forehead. He moved his eyes to the right and saw Anne. It was the first close view he'd had of her since she kissed him. Drops of his blood ran down her face.

He said, "I'd like to stand. The snow is as cold as hell, and my ass is freezing." He smiled at her.

Anne jumped up and ran back into the burning house. An instant later she was out again and running back through the snow to him.

"Take this. It will help keep your ass warm." She wrapped a warm blanket around his shoulders and kissed his cheek.

"I feel better already." He smiled. "Now, please, let me stand. This is very undignified. I'm supposed to be in charge here."

"All right, the ambulance is coming down the street, anyway," Mettler said. "If you can get up, we'll walk to the curb and meet them." Then Mettler yelled, "Flemming, put Mr. Charon in a car, but make sure you search him first."

Anne and Mettler helped Niall to his feet as the ambulance and fire engines pulled up in front of the house. The paramedics took Niall, and Anne followed them into the ambulance.

"There goes what's left of my life," she said to Niall.

"I'm sorry about this, Anne."

"It's hard to watch your life disappear, but if it weren't for you, I'd be lying out there in the snow too."

"Life never turns out exactly the way we plan, does it?"

"I suppose not."

"He's a lucky guy," one of the EMTs said to Mettler, "but we'll have to take him to the hospital."

"Tell the Sergeant I'd like a word with him," Niall said to the paramedic.

As Mettler hoisted his huge body back inside the ambulance, Anne went back outside and watched her house burn, despite attempts by the firefighters to get control of the flames.

"What is it, sir?"

"I don't think I'm going to be in any condition to work in the morning, and I'm not sure the Chief will even want me around, but you have to go to Joe Madera's autopsy. I have a feeling about it."

Mettler graced Niall with one of his rare smiles. "I'll take care of it. I'll come see you as soon as everything is cleared up here." Mettler looked out the back of the ambulance. "The Chief just arrived."

"Thanks, Anthony. Remember: You were only following my orders."

"You saved her life, sir. That counts for a lot."

The paramedic checked his eyes with a flashlight, then cleaned the wound on the right side of his head. Niall thought about Maggie. He could still smell her hair. He wondered if he'd been close to death or if it was just a dream.

"Why are you looking at me that way?"

Niall focused his eyes and saw Anne's face above him. He wanted to smell her hair; perhaps the scent was hers. "I'm sorry, I was thinking about something from my past."

"Was it Maggie again?"

Niall was startled. "Are you the one doing the mindreading now?"

"No, you called her name when you were lying on me. I don't mind telling you that under different circumstances, I would be greatly offended."

"If I were conscious, I can assure you you'd receive my full attention." He forced a smile through the throbbing pain in his head. "How are you feeling?"

"Numb. My whole life is gone, even that stupid bottle of Calvados. I'm not sure anymore what it represented to me. The only things I have left are these two photo albums." She held them up for him to see.

A tear rolled down her face and fell to his lips. She wiped it away but some had already made its way to his taste buds.

"We're ready now, close the doors," one of the paramedics said.

A fourth person climbed into the ambulance and the doors closed. It was Flemming.

"I was watching you, Flemming. You did a good job," Niall said.

"Thank you, sir." She said to Anne, "You're tougher than I thought, Miss Tadmore."

"Back at you, Officer Flemming."

The ambulance pulled out into the deepening snow. Niall watched the flames and the flashing lights out the back window until the white night swallowed them.

* * *

CHAPTER XIX

The storm lasted a day and a half. A three-foot layer of white powder blanketed the tri-state area and closed everything for two days.

Niall was still in the hospital and felt like a prisoner. He suspected that the Chief had arranged with Dr. Whitley to keep him there. Every time he asked if he could leave, Whitley would study his chart, smile, and then say he needed to stay another day or two. Niall wasn't happy with his confinement. He felt as close to normal as ever and being hospitalized while the killer roamed free wasn't easy to tolerate. The nurse stormed into his room, took his vitals, and asked how he was feeling, always with the same indifferent tone. He contemplated inventing a story, but simply surrendered to the rules and attempted to enjoy his forced vacation. His mother and uncle called again from Ireland to check on him. He told them repeatedly that he was fine, but his mother insisted he find a respectable line of work, or come back to Ireland and find a nice girl to marry, while his uncle told him to give up the foolishness and write poetry. Niall was tempted to tell him about his aisling poem, but he'd spent too many summers with Ciarán instructing him in the way of the poet to say anything before it was done.

Niall recalled the carnage that had plagued his dreams the entire first night; fortunately, the nurses had kept waking him to make sure he was O.K. The image of Dr. Prabdha smiling recurred repeatedly in his mind, but he didn't understand why that particular image was so strong, though it seemed such an incongruous thing to be doing while his arm was burning. Niall hypothesized that Prabdha was smiling because cremation was his preferred method of burial, but when he couldn't find a more rational solution, he forced the image away by concentrating on Maggie, or Anne's kiss, or the taste of her tear on his lips. He wondered why the good images were harder to remember than the bad ones. Still, the memories were fading – and in place of them came guilt. He berated himself for not acting sooner. He should have stopped Prabdha as soon as Anne let him and Billy Ananda through the door. They would be alive, and Sara and Anne would still have a home.

Chief Pack had stopped by that first night to tell him how he'd displayed a bad lapse of judgment when he came up with his 'ridiculously inappropriate and unprofessional scheme, that he knew better than to play fast-and-loose with the rules, and it was a lucky thing Mettler had been with him. Of course, there'd have to be a full investigation and until then, Niall was on restricted duty. Niall expected he'd be suspended or maybe even lose his job.

The Chief took off on a tangent about the media having a field day; they were calling the town the new murder capital of the country. He ranted about the budget and what would they do if Anne and Sara decided to sue. Niall tried to calm Pack down by saying Sara was still missing and probably would be happy just to live through her ordeal, but that only infuriated the Chief further. The town's insurance premiums would skyrocket; the mayor and the members of the town council had been telephoning him endlessly for updates. Two more foreign nationals were dead, and the Indian government wanted a full explanation. Niall replied that as soon as they recovered the sapphires, the Indian government would forget about the situation. A few million dollars had a way of calming people. The Chief told him not to be so sure.

Thanks to Herzog's broadcast, the word had gotten around that Niall was involved with Anne. The Chief had liked that news even less, though Niall told him it wasn't true. It didn't matter; Chief Pack ordered him not to talk to her again.

All in all, it hadn't gone as badly as it might have. Sure, the Chief yelled, but when he yelled too loudly, Niall grabbed his head and grimaced in pain. Mettler had reminded everyone, that Niall had saved Anne's life, though the house was a total loss. Pack seemed to think that the property counted more than her life.

Sara was still missing, and Niall worried about her constantly. He swore to himself that he'd get her back safely in spite of being on restricted duty. Peter Drago and Mike Rodriguez were still missing too, and no one had heard anything about the elusive Sammy Sloan. He still had one card up his sleeve and was waiting to play it, although, the Chief had ordered Mettler not to discuss the case with Niall. Niall only wanted to know one thing: the results of Joe Madera's autopsy.

It was Thursday. Mettler's wife was returning after her two-week visit to her family in California; Mettler was stopping to see Niall on his way to the airport.

Tommy Cordero's funeral was that morning. Niall knew Anne was determined to pay her last respects. All of her belongings had been destroyed and he wanted her to have something decent to wear. He thought of asking Flemming to help him, but he remembered Anne saying that Flemming had a crush on him, so Niall asked Mettler to buy several items of clothing for Anne. Mettler had grumbled and told Niall he was asking for trouble, but Niall promised to come to the dinner his wife had been trying to arrange to set him up with a friend. Niall decided it would be worth it to see Anne in nice clothes. The green parka might keep her warm, but it didn't do much for her looks. He asked Maxwell Good, who was being released that morning, to give the clothes to Anne, so she would believe they were a gift from him. Niall felt satisfied with the plan until he remembered how his last one hadn't turned out too well.

A dull thud of a knock on the door brought a smile to his face. He'd grown accustomed to the frequent visits of his new friend.

"Come in, Maxwell."

"I'm almost sorry to be leaving here. The nurses are good company, and I've enjoyed my time with you and Anne."

"You're lucky. I feel like a prisoner. Look at you, very stylish. Where'd you find that fancy black suit? If it weren't for your purple hair and long beard, you could be a bank president."

"Why, thank you. I do try to blend as much as possible into modern society but not all the way." Good ran a bandaged hand across his hair.

"How are the hands?"

"They work – and they don't look too bad, either. I just left the ever-brusque Dr. Whitley. He gave me a clean bill of health. I can take the bandages off in two days; I'll be painting in three."

"Bravo, maestro! But where are you going to paint?"

"Oh, I have a few houses scattered around and, besides, all I need are some brushes, paint, canvas, and I'm ready to go."

"You have 'a few houses'?" Niall asked with astonishment.

"You must have guessed that I wasn't poor."

"Yes, but I didn't do a financial background check on you."

"I have an apartment-slash-studio in Manhattan, another one in Paris, a nice place in San Francisco, and my parents' big old house here in town. You may use any of them you like, and for as long as you like – provided, of course, that I'm not entertaining a friend and that you don't burn them down. In fact, you might feel the need to get away from here after the events of the last week."

"That's really generous of you, Maxwell, but I have a few loose ends to wrap up before my boss completely blockades my involvement."

"I already invited Anne to go to Paris for a few months. You can go with her if you like. There's more than enough room for two." He winked at Niall.

Niall smiled. "Maybe later. The situation isn't completely clear yet. Sara and the two young men are still missing and there's a funeral to attend."

"If you don't like Paris, you can stay in my place on the west coast or in Manhattan."

Niall didn't know if Good was playing matchmaker or just a generous person, but he didn't like being indebted to people. His mother had put the fear of God in him about taking charity after his father died, so he still felt uneasy about offers. 'People don't give nothing for nothing,' his mother always told him.

"Thanks Maxwell. You're not leaving now, are you? Sergeant Mettler hasn't arrived with the packages."

"No, not right away. I thought I'd present them to Anne when I go to say goodbye."

Shortly after Maxwell left, Mettler entered with four shopping bags.

"I'm sorry I'm running so late, sir. I won't even tell you what I had to go through to buy these clothes."

Niall jumped out of bed to inspect Mettler's purchases. The first bag contained beautiful black leather boots. Another contained a long black cashmere coat and a matching beret. The third bag held a black wool dress, stockings, a scarf, black bra and panties. The last one contained the bulletproof vest Niall had requested.

Mettler said, "Sir, I don't mind telling you that I think the bullet must have damaged your brain. I can't believe you're willing to spend so much on her."

"I'll explain my reasoning to you one of these days. I think you'll understand how important it is to me when you hear the story."

Mettler pulled a folded sheet of paper out of his pocket, then hesitated.

Niall asked, "Was I right?"

Mettler handed him the paper without saying anything.

Niall read the autopsy report and handed it back to him.

"I don't like that look in your eye, sir." Mettler glanced at his wristwatch. "I have to go to the airport and meet my wife. Please wait until I get back. Remember, the Chief ordered you to stay out of it, and I already told my wife you'd come to dinner, so I'll never hear the end of it if you get yourself killed."

"Anthony, you worry too much. I don't even have my weapon. What kind of trouble can I get into? I'm only going to take Anne to the boy's funeral."

Mettler gave him a distrustful look.

"I'll pick up my wife, then meet you at the cemetery as soon as I can. By the way, I ran into a rather unpleasant Gennifer Bidon when she came to pay her respects to Joe Madera."

"Did they let her see him?"

"I think so."

"Shit. Did you question her?"

"I didn't have time."

"Anthony, Anthony, Anthony. Tell your wife to set the date for the dinner. I'll be there. You have my word on it."

"You're much too happy, sir. Maybe I should stay here with you. My wife would understand."

"Get out of here." Niall gently shoved the puzzled Mettler out the door.

Niall washed up, finished dressing, then opened the door. Flemming was in her usual position outside Anne's door. Her demeanor had changed. The violence and death had softened her. She wasn't a rookie anymore.

"Hi, L.T. You're not leaving, are you?"

"I'm looking for Mr. Good. Is he still around?"

"He's talking to Miss Tadmore, sir."

"Would you tell him I'd like to see him when he comes out?"

"Yes, sir."

Niall went back to his room and took his notebook from his inside pocket. He read the Aisling. It was almost finished. He studied it to make sure all the words were just how he wanted. A knock on the door interrupted his scribbling.

Flemming stuck her head in the door. "Are you all right, sir?"

"I'm perfect. Why do you ask?"

"It's just that I've never seen you with such a big grin on your face."

"I'll try and keep my smiles to myself in the future, Flemming. Is that all?"

"I'm leaving now, sir. The Chief ordered us back to the station. He said the budget couldn't handle any more overtime, but

I think it's really because Mr. Good has been released. I hope I get the chance to work with you again, sir. I learned a lot."

"I hope so too."

She closed the door.

His future with the department was still up in the air. Maybe he seemed too happy, but he couldn't and didn't want to control the happiness right now. Lightness had infused him since seeing Maggie. He realized a few days ago that he'd been waiting most of his life to finish the poem, and he was near the end. Maybe the dreams about his father would also stop when the poem was complete. This poem could be the catharsis he needed to reconcile his past.

The familiar rat-tat-tat knock preceded Maxwell Good's return and Niall.

"How's she doing?" Niall asked.

"She's fine. Did someone smuggle you some joy juice?"

"I know, I'm way too happy. You're the third person who's told me this morning. I truly appreciate your doing this for me, Maxwell." Niall handed him the bags.

"I don't understand you young people, but I'm the one who'll probably get a hug and a kiss, so I don't care."

"Take care of yourself, Maxwell. I'll see you around town."

"You have my number. Don't be a stranger."

* * *

CHAPTER XX

Niall waited fifteen long minutes, worrying that Anne would be killed. He didn't know if he would be able to live with that consequence, but he was determined to take her to the cemetery. He put on his overcoat, checked the small bandage on his head, then went next door. When he opened Anne's door without knocking, she was standing in the middle of the room wearing only the new black panties.

"Oh! Excuse me. I came to see you, but I...I didn't expect to see so much of you. I'll wait outside." His face flushed, but he didn't move to leave as fast as he could have.

"Sure, fine," she replied without any apparent embarrassment.

He stepped out, the image of her well-proportioned breasts, strong legs and flat stomach tattooed on his memory. Niall was glad Flemming was gone. She'd already seen him smiling; he didn't want her to see him drooling as well.

Another few minutes went by before Anne said, "You can come in now, Lieutenant."

Niall opened the door. "I'm sorry for not knocking. I guess I wasn't thinking."

She smiled and did a few turns, marveling at her new self in front of the bathroom mirror. Niall felt a sense of accomplishment.

Anne looked beautiful even without make-up. She resembled Maggie even more now – but she wasn't Maggie. Now that he'd seen her naked, he knew their differences.

Anne walked over to stand very close to him. Niall concentrated on her moist lips.

"What are you looking at? Do I have dirt on my face?"

"No, I'm sorry. I didn't mean to stare."

"Well then, what do you think?" She pirouetted in place to show him. "This outfit was a present from Maxwell."

"You look beautiful."

Their eyes met, then he looked away. He didn't know why he couldn't meet her gaze. Her eyes looked cold, and made him nervous. Maybe it was the guilt of what he was about to do.

"How are you feeling?" Anne asked.

Niall focused his eyes on the movements of her mouth. "I'm well," he replied.

"Are you sure? You look feverish." She placed her cool hand on his forehead.

"No, I'm absolutely healthy."

"Good. I also have the impression, from all the officials who came to question me that you're in trouble, Lieutenant."

Her fragrance drifted to his nostrils. "I thought we had a deal. You were going to call me Niall, and I would call you Anne."

"O.K., Niall, are you in trouble?"

"I wouldn't call it trouble, but things didn't turn out as neatly as I had envisioned. And I wasn't totally honest with the chief about what we were doing."

"What did you tell him?"

"That's the issue: I didn't tell him anything. Everything would have gone perfectly if Mr. Charon hadn't shown up and thrown the bottle. His arrival complicated the issue. Mettler and the detectives were waiting outside for all of you to walk out the door. We would have arrested the Doctor and Billy Ananda without any incident."

"So they blamed you for my house burning down and the two dead men?"

"The Chief is still investigating, which means he's consulting with the attorneys to see how much liability the town has."

"He's afraid someone will sue?"

"Everyone sues whenever they think there's a few dollars to be made. It's the American way."

"What about Martin? What's going to happen to him?"

"I haven't been privy to all the information, but Mettler told me that Mr. Charon hasn't said a word since the other night, though he giggles every so often. I don't know if he's lost his mind or if he's just playing games. Anyway, the D.A. decided to let the federal government prosecute him, so they shipped him to New York. I think the Justice Department is trying to figure out what to prosecute him for. If Charon is smart enough, and gets himself a good lawyer, he could probably cut a deal – that is if there is anyone left, he could roll over on. Then again, they might not be able to find enough evidence to convict him."

Anne sat down on the bed.

"Do you still have feelings for Charon?" he asked.

"I don't know. I've thought more over the last few days than I've done in a long time. The last week has given me a new perspective on life and the way I've been dealing with it. I realize how short life can be. I'm not going to waste any more of it. I'm going to do everything I ever wanted to do. I'm not putting off my dreams until later. Maxwell invited Sara and me to stay at his place in Paris; I intend to go as soon as we find her."

Niall saw tears forming in her eyes. He wasn't sure if he should be doing what he was about to do, but he didn't see any other way out. The Chief was a good man, but his priorities were different: He was worried about an entire department and a city. Niall had only himself to worry about. If this didn't work out, he would go back to Ireland; his mother and uncle would be happy to have him home. The happiness he'd felt earlier faded under the weight of what he was about to do.

"I came to escort you to Tommy's funeral," he said.

"I never thought about suing." She wiped her eyes with a tissue. "Well, I'm relieved they're letting me go to the funeral."

Her shoulders dropped a little lower. Niall wanted to hug her. Nothing ever stays the same, he thought, as a momentary sadness descended on him.

Niall held the door open for her. She put on the black coat, then picked up the ratty sweatshirt.

"Are you bringing that with you?"

"It's sort of a security blanket." Anne pulled the faded gray sweatshirt to her chest as she walked out of the room. "Where are Flemming and the other officers?"

"The Chief decided the overtime was breaking the budget, so he sent them home."

"The hospital won't be the same without her smiling face," Anne replied with a grin.

They walked straight to the car Mettler had left for him. Niall didn't tell anyone they were leaving. He felt vulnerable without his weapon. He knew the killer was still out there waiting for Anne.

"If your boss doesn't want to spend the money to protect me, think how he'll feel when my lawyer files suit against the department."

"Relax, I won't let anything happen to you – and if you do decide to sue the town, don't tell the Chief it was me who planted the bee in your bonnet." Niall stuck a tape in the cassette player. "This'll help calm you."

The sweet voice of a traditional Irish singer accompanied them on the short ride to Calvary cemetery. Anne told Niall that her parents, and Sara's father, were buried there and it was where she saw Martin for the first time. Although Niall didn't volunteer the information, Maggie was there now, too.

"I haven't heard anything about Joe's funeral," Anne said.

"The Medical Examiner has been completing tests, but I'm sure something will happen soon."

Anne nodded. "I guess I'll be attending funerals for a while. Do you think this is how older people feel when all of their friends start dying?" She had an intensely unhappy air about her.

"Don't be so morose. Try to think of something happy. Think about your trip to Paris with Sara and Maxwell."

"I think it's about time you fulfilled your promise," she replied.

"What promise are you referring to?"

"C'mon, Niall, you remember. I want to hear the poem."

"I was hoping the stress had knocked all of that out of your memory."

"Either out with the poem, or stop so I can call my lawyer."

"Can you wait a little longer? It's not quite finished."

"How much longer is it going to take you to write it? You've been in the hospital for days."

Niall ignored her; he didn't know how long it would take. A murderer was lurking out there somewhere – although, it was possible the killer would just slip away into obscurity, perhaps having decided killing Anne wasn't worth the trouble. What if they never found Sara?

"There's the cemetery and it looks like there's quite a crowd," he said.

"Is that a television news truck up there?"

"Yes, several of them. You've become famous. Sergeant Mettler said they've had calls asking about you since Monday night. They all want to interview you, and some have been offering a lot of money for the chance."

"I don't want to go," she said abruptly. Take me back to the hospital."

"Anne, you can't hide forever."

"I'm not hiding. All they want is another disaster so they can increase their viewing audience. I've been watching the news, I hear what they're calling me: *'Disaster Girl does it again. Who will be the next victim of the Deadly Damsel?'* Please! Don't make me go there. I'll sign a paper saying I won't sue the city. I still have a few things I haven't told you; I'll come clean. Just don't make me face those cameras."

"I thought you wanted to pay your last respects to Tommy."

"I do, but not with the entire world watching. Look at it – it's a circus over there. Let's go to my parents' grave instead. Please, Niall! I'll even forget your promise, so you don't have to tell me the poem. What do you say?"

Niall wasn't sure about taking her to a more secluded spot. He had been counting on the crowd to give the killer a sense of security.

He sighed. "I'll take you to visit your parents' grave and then we're going back to the hospital. Tell me what information you've been withholding."

Anne slumped as they drove by the vehicles scattered alongside the road, but most of the people were up the hill near the gravesite. No one paid attention to the lone car as it passed.

Anne took an automatic pistol out of her sweatshirt and handed it to him.

"My, my, how long have you been carrying this around with you?" he asked.

"Since Sunday night. I found it in the pocket of my parka before we left the hospital on Monday. It was Tommy's."

"It didn't do him much good, did it?"

"I suppose not."

"What else have you been hiding?"

"I knew Martin was in the house the other day." She paused for him to respond but he didn't. "I found him hiding in the large cabinet when I went into the kitchen to turn on the lights and fix a cup of tea."

Niall remembered the squeal she'd made the other night.

"Was he the mouse you told me you saw?"

"Yes, I'm sorry. I should have told you."

Mettler, no fool, had questioned Anne about Martin's sudden appearance, but she'd denied knowing he was there. Niall had suspected she'd lied; he no longer felt completely to blame for the deaths of Dr. Prabdha and Billy Ananda.

"Tell me what happened."

"Martin put his hand over my mouth and pulled me close to him when I opened the kitchen cupboard. He swore he had nothing to do with the killings. He said all he ever wanted were the stupid keys. He looked so pitiful when I told him I threw them away. He giggled like an idiot. I had convinced him to give himself up when you yelled for me to come to the living room. Martin slipped back into the closet to wait it out. He was a mess; I felt sorry for him, and I didn't see what harm he could do squatting in there. I didn't know he'd come out and throw my bottle of Calvados."

Niall drove slowly around the perimeter of the cemetery without saying a word. He was simultaneously relieved and furious. If Anne had told him about Martin, her house wouldn't have been burned and two people would probably still be alive.

She read his mind. "It's all my fault, isn't it?"

It was, but Niall didn't want to make her feel worse than she already did.

"Don't you think it's ironic that he helped you to acquire your taste for Calvados, and then he used it to burn your house to the ground?"

"Next, you'll be saying it has a certain poetic justice to it. I don't think it's ironic. All that Sara and I had was in that house. I don't even know if I'll ever see Sara again."

Anne wrapped her arms around herself. It was the same defensive posture she was in the first time he saw her.

Niall was confused and a bit disappointed. "What did you expect me to do, Anne? I'm not going to yell at you. I just wish you had told me he was there."

"I'm sorry. What else can I say? The newspapers are right. You can park on that side," she said, pointing to the left. "Their grave is a little way up the hill."

Niall followed her directions but didn't turn off the engine.

He said, "I suppose this could wait until later, but I might as well tell you now. Sgt. Mettler told me they discovered that Charon was sleeping with the wife of the Dean of Humanities while the Dean was at some conference. Martin must have left Sara unconscious in the bed after she hit her head, probably assuming she would go home when she woke. Someone else came along and put her in the closet."

"Do we have to go over this now?"

"No, but I thought we were clearing our consciences."

"That's very thoughtful of you, Lieutenant, but I don't want to hear any more now. I'd just like to visit my parents' grave for a few minutes."

He felt guilty again – now, for not knowing when to keep his mouth shut.

Niall said, "The hillside is almost devoid of human interference."

"You mean there aren't many footprints in the snow?"

"That's exactly what I mean. Some, but not many. It looks very beautiful, doesn't it? The sun is shining. The sky and the air are crystal-clear. Snow still clings to the sides of the trees and it is pure white with only the gray shadows of the tombstones falling on it and the yellow glow of the sun."

"Are we having a poetic moment, Lieutenant?"

He turned to her with a smile, "You're calling me Lieutenant again. I'm sorry that I upset you."

"I'll be back in a few minutes, Lieutenant. I'm off to defile the pure white snow with my gray shadow and my human interference."

"You're not off to defile anything without me. I'm not leaving you alone out in the open."

He picked up the automatic, checked to make sure the clip was full, and slipped the weapon into his coat pocket. Then he opened his door and stepped onto the slippery road; Anne got out too. The path was covered with snow but made passable by some earlier visitors.

She walked carefully around to his side of the car. "I hope these new boots are waterproof. I'd hate to ruin such a wonderful gift the first time I wear them."

She promptly slipped on a patch of ice. Niall caught her by the arm and pulled her close to him. She smiled and put her arms around him.

"Thanks, Niall."

"You're not angry at me anymore?"

"I'm mostly angry at myself. You're right, I should have told you. I didn't think anyone was going to come to the house and then it all became so real. Afterwards, I was afraid to say anything. Am I in trouble?"

"I don't know. Don't tell anyone about talking to Charon until I think about it. Come along, it's getting colder. Let's go up the hill and visit your parents."

"Right. I'll lead the way." She took him by the hand.

Niall liked holding her hand but didn't feel right about it. He self-consciously scanned the hillside. There was no one in sight. The two-day-old snow crunched under their feet as they passed rows of headstones – some were taller than him and shaped like crosses, others were so small, they were mostly buried under snow. They reached an area with mausoleums built in the 1920s and '30s.

"It's not far now," Anne said, as they passed one of the larger ones.

"I think that's far enough," replied a male voice.

* * *

CHAPTER XXI

"What?" Anne stopped and turned to Niall.

"I said I think that's far enough, Anne. Don't move, Lieutenant. Keep your hands where I can see them."

Niall and Anne swiveled in the direction of the voice. The black metal doorway of the mausoleum framed Joe Madera.

"Joe? I though you were dead!" Anne said.

"Sorry to disappoint you, but I'm not dead yet. Actually, the odds are in my favor that I'll outlive you all." He leveled a small-caliber pistol at them. "Come out here, Sara."

Sara walked from the shadows of the mausoleum. Her hands were tied behind her back, she had a white rag stuffed in her mouth, held in place by gray duct tape, her face was red and she was obviously having difficulty breathing.

Madera pushed her toward them.

"Here we are all together again. One nice happy family – and with the Lieutenant as a special guest," he smirked.

"I was wondering when you'd show up," Niall said to Madera.

Anne hit Niall in the arm. "You knew? You knew he wasn't dead and you didn't tell me?"

"Sorry."

"Isn't that sweet? Anne and Niall sitting in a tree," Madera mocked. He waved the pistol back and forth between them. "How could you be expecting me to show up? I'm dead, Lieutenant."

"Your plan might have worked, except that the body of your friend Mr. Sloan didn't burn completely. He thought very highly of himself and had his back tattooed. Would you like to know what it said?" Niall asked, keeping his voice level trying to maintain calm, as Madera was several steps beyond Niall's reach.

Niall noticed a woman making her way through the snow toward them. He watched her slow methodical plodding steps over Madera's right shoulder.

Madera said, "I shouldn't have propped him in front of the door, but it doesn't matter. The three of you won't be around much longer," he chuckled. "By the way, I read about your heroic act, Lieutenant. Too bad it didn't do you any good. I hear you might lose your job. Did they take your gun?"

"Yes." Niall opened his coat and made a full circle to show Madera that he was unarmed, hoping he didn't notice the bulge in his coat pocket – or the approaching woman.

"That moron Sammy couldn't do the simple job I paid him to do. All he had to do was throw a beating on that asshole Charon. When he went to the house, he found Sara on the bed, but not Charon. Stupid Sammy Sloan raped her, then tied her up in the closet naked just because she'd blown him off."

"So you paid Sammy to beat up Charon. Is that what started this mess?" Niall asked, still stalling, while hoping the approaching woman would distract Madera long enough for him to retrieve the gun from his pocket.

"I just told you I did, didn't I? Talk about coincidences. We met in the bar at Sammie's restaurant. You remember that place, don't you, Anne?" He waved the pistol in her direction. "The only reason he went there was because his first name was Sammy, and it made him feel important. He said, 'This is Sammie's, and I'm a Sammy too.' What a dope."

Niall glanced at Anne. Her face was red, but he couldn't tell if it was from cold, confusion, or rage.

"What's the matter, Anne – can't stand the truth? Well, you might as well hear it all. We got drunk, and he told me his life story. He'd never done anything in his life, and all the world was against him, blah, blah, blah. Man did he go on about how life had mistreated him. He was wallowing in his shit more than I was. He told me he'd just lost his job because of some bitch house painter. Oh yeah, that caught my attention. Boy, did my ears tingle when he said that. I couldn't resist asking him which house-painting bitch had cost him his job, then the whole unsavory story about his date with Sara and the bitch came out. He believed Anne turned Sara against him. I told him about Martin and you, Anne, and how I'd like a little revenge. I knew he wasn't functioning on all cylinders, but what the heck. I decided to use his mental incompetence to my benefit. I offered him two hundred dollars to hurt Charon. He needed money; I needed some kind of satisfaction, and some kind of release. Unfortunately, I didn't realize how empty-headed he was."

Anne asked. "Joe, why didn't you come talk to me?"

"Shit, Anne. How many times did we talk about the future? How many times did I ask you to marry me? How many times did you say you weren't ready for marriage? Then you walked all over me for six months before you dropped me completely. You never heard a single word I ever said. What good would it have done? Tell me."

"We can work it out, Joe, it's not too late. You don't have to hurt anyone else."

"You're not listening again, Anne. It is too late. It was too late last week. I won't spend the rest of my life in jail."

"Sara and the Lieutenant haven't done anything to you. Please, let them go."

"You should have been more considerate last year. We might have had a good life." He aimed the pistol at her.

"JOE! Why did Sammy wait almost three days to go after Anne?" Niall asked loudly, pulling Joe's attention away from Anne.

Joe stopped and studied him for a long minute. Niall could see the wheels turning inside his head. Joe chuckled and lowered the pistol for a split-second, but not long enough for Niall to make a move.

"Instead of leaving town like he was going to do, the idiot went on a drinking binge, so by Friday he was even more out of his mind than usual. I hadn't heard anything about Charon in the news and began to wonder. I even had some second thoughts because I was drunk when I made the deal with Sammy, but it was already too late."

Anne stomped her feet in the snow and was beginning to shake. Sara, on Niall's right, was barely able to stand; she was shaking violently and sucking air hard through her nostrils. The woman trudging through the snow was much closer to them – and Niall knew who she was from her bright red hair. She changed direction to use the mausoleums as cover so that Madera wouldn't be able to see her until she was right on top of him.

Madera shook his head and his face contorted with rage, but then he calmed himself and continued.

"Sammy went back on Friday night to see if Sara was still in the house. He wanted to do her again, but the police were already there. He saw Anne leaving with a detective, and decided to go to her house and do the same to her, but Sammy didn't have a car, so he walked, stopping at every bar on the way. When he finally reached the house, he saw Charon in the backyard with some little Indian guy. He waited until Charon and the Indian left, then Sammy slipped in the back door and went to Anne's bedroom – just in time to see her driving away. A few minutes later, the Indian guy came back. Sammy knocked him out, then searched him and found a gun. He took it, along with the guy's wallet and his car keys. He was so pissed that Anne had slipped out of his hands that he dragged the guy from the kitchen into her room and shot him." Madera let out another laugh that would have scared the dead.

Sara's face turned white. Niall tried not to be distracted by the women, but Sara was shaking uncontrollably and Anne kept shuffling her feet. She appeared to be desperately searching for a way to appease Joe, but Niall knew Madera was way beyond reason.

"Anyway, after Sammy called the cops from Anne's room, he found the guy's car. I think he believed the police would actually bust Anne for the murder. A short time later he called me, told me what happened, then demanded five thousand dollars, or he'd tell the police it was all my idea. I agreed to meet him."

Niall saw a tiny puff of frozen breath come from behind the corner of a mausoleum two down from where they stood. Gennifer Bidon walked out from behind it and took a step toward them, trying not to make any noise, but a man's arm reached out from behind the mausoleum, covered her mouth with his large hand and pulled her back behind the building. Niall recognized Sergeant Mettler's coat and almost laughed.

"Gennifer Bidon didn't mention that phone call when I spoke with her," Niall said.

"She was in the shower. I would have taken care of that little pig too, if I could have made sure it got blamed on Anne. You don't know what she put me through – talk about sexual harassment!"

Madera seemed to lose his train of thought and Niall wondered how long it had been since he'd slept, but he had a look of determination on his face that chilled Niall to his core.

"Then what happened? When did Anne call you?" Niall asked.

"What? Oh yeah. Anne asked me for a place to stay. I didn't know that the pig answered the call. God, is she awful in bed! Not like you, Anne." He waved the pistol in her direction.

Niall wondered if Anthony was alone. It wasn't likely, but what was his plan? Joe could get off several shots before Niall reached the automatic in his pocket, so he needed either a sign from Mettler or a distraction.

"How did you decide to use Maxwell's place?" Niall asked.

"Maxwell?" Madera laughed. "He owed me a favor. Did he tell you I saved his life?"

"Yes, he did."

"His studio was sort of isolated, which I figured might come in handy. As the day wore on, it became clear to me that even if I gave Sammy the money, he'd want more as soon as he'd spent it, and if he were caught, he'd still blame the whole thing on me. Regardless of whether I could be charged with the murder, it would be the end of my life. What kind of job could I get after

I got out of jail? Tell me. Could I become a cop? Or maybe a lawyer? Do you think Gennifer would hold my job at the hotel until I was released? Answer me, Lieutenant, or I'll shoot Sara." Madera aimed the pistol at her.

"That isn't necessary, Joe. You're right. I don't suppose you could find a job as a policeman or a lawyer. I think Gennifer would hold your job for you, though."

"No hotel would want an ex-felon running one of their operations. The only way for me to escape was to die. I thought about killing myself, and then I had a better idea."

"You killed two birds with one stone," Niall said.

"That's right. The whole thing was tricky to arrange, but I was sure I'd worked out all the details, down to the smallest item. I would have made a great hotel manager or CEO."

"Too bad you didn't check Sammy for identifying marks and tattoos before you blew him up. We were looking for him."

"Sammy was an idiot and eventually would have killed someone else – or himself. The world won't miss him." Madera lowered the gun for a second to rest his arm, then raised it again. "I still can't believe all of this is real. Anne, tell me this is a dream, and I'm going to wake up in bed next to you."

Anne looked from Joe to Niall. "I'm sorry, Joe. I wish I could make it all right, but your killing us isn't going to make it go away either."

"I know, but I have enough money stashed to have a great time before anyone finds me. Don't look so worried, Anne. I'd like for you to be the last one to die. You can watch both dear Sara and your new beau Niall die before your turn comes."

A small red point of light appeared on the mausoleum wall behind Madera. It was the sign Niall had been waiting for.

He said casually, as if they were having a harmless chat, "There are policemen around us with rifles. Please don't make any sudden moves."

Madera surveyed the area. "Always the cop, aren't you? I don't see anyone," he said, but his voice betrayed uncertainty. He lowered the gun from exhaustion and then raised it again.

Niall knew he didn't have much time before Madera would start shooting. "Of course you don't see them. Would you be here now if you had seen them?" Niall raised his voice. "Sergeant, would you show Mr. Madera that I'm not bluffing?"

Two spots of red light appeared on Madera's chest. The blood drained from his face as he recognized the meaning.

After a second, he said, "You think you've got me, don't you?"

"I only see two ways out for you. Why don't you hand me the gun and we can talk about it," Niall said, extending his left hand.

Madera smirked, then turned deadly serious. "I never intended to hurt Maxwell; he's always been a good friend to me."

Anne said, "Joe, please don't hurt anyone else. Think of the good times we had together. They far outweigh the bad times."

The sound of her voice had the same effect as setting a match to gasoline.

"You bitch," Madera said as he fired.

Niall pulled Anne toward him but she grabbed her left shoulder and dropped to the ground. Before Niall could push Sara out of the way and grab for the automatic, a second shot rang out.

Madera dropped to the snow with a bullet hole in the center of his forehead.

Niall took the gun from Madera's hand and went to check Anne. Once again, she was lucky. The bullet had only nicked her shoulder.

"Just stay still," he said. "An ambulance will be here soon."

"He shot me. I can't believe he shot me," Anne said.

"It's over. He's dead."

Niall untied Sara as Sergeant Mettler, Gennifer Bidon, and four SWAT team members arrived.

Gennifer Bidon slumped into the snow in tears.

"I thought you were going to the airport," Niall said to Mettler.

"I was until you volunteered as a decoy to trap Madera. I told the Chief what you said and he agreed that it was a good way for you to redeem yourself. He asked me to coordinate the stakeout. Lucky for you that Mr. Madera liked to talk; it gave us the time to position the team."

"Indeed. What about your wife?"

"My brother went to get her. He owed me a favor."

"I don't know how to thank you."

"You can come to dinner next week."

Niall smiled. "I'll be there."

Two ambulances arrived, and the EMTs began treating Anne and Sara. Sergeant Mettler directed the officers to seal off the area, as the news crews from Tommy Cordero's funeral began pulling up at the bottom of the hill.

Niall stood back from the crowd.

Mettler reappeared at his side.

"We found Peter Drago and Mike Rodriguez further up the hill at Charon's family mausoleum. They were looking for the sapphires but didn't find them."

"We'll see if the Feds can convince Charon to tell them where he hid them. Meanwhile, we caught the bad guys and saved the fairy princesses."

"I don't get it, Niall," Mettler said.

Niall smiled. "We did our job. Let's go fill out reports."

He clapped Mettler on the back and they walked down the hill.

* * *

CHAPTER XXII

Niall returned to his office after leaving Anne, Sara, and Maxwell Good at JFK airport, off on their big trip to Paris. Anne was in search of Calvados; she and Sara, with the help of Maxwell Good, were going to study art. Maxwell told Niall he liked the excitement of being around them because it made his creative juices flow. Niall understood what he meant. His life didn't feel the same without them. It had been five weeks since he walked into Martin Charon's kitchen and saw the angry Anne for the first time. They probably weren't even on the plane yet and he already felt a bit emptier.

As a going away present, Anne had given him a scrapbook with all the newspaper clippings about him, her and the case. He wondered if maybe she were trying to make up for all of the chaos she'd caused. There had been so much confusion after the cemetery scene. Chief Pack had told him to keep away from Anne. Niall didn't obey the Chief that often and wondered why he'd done it this time. He still thought a lot about Maggie, the dream about his father, and the poem. Maybe that was why he hadn't asked Anne out.

He also wondered why he had given in to her demands for his poem. He remembered telling her when she was in the hospital he would show it to her, but he'd never thought she would be so persistent. Mettler still maintained that Niall had a crush on her, and should have asked her out. Was he right? Niall remembered her standing naked, the way she'd looked at him as he studied her, and how she'd kissed him at the airport. He didn't know exactly why he hadn't asked her out but she'd be back.

One cold winter morning,
before the birds began to sing
a troubled woman appeared to me.
The film of sleep clung to my eyes, and
my spirit fought to break the spell.

Trapped, I listened.
Hesitant, she began her tale
and the words dripped slowly,
like cold honey, from her ruby lips.
Her green eyes sparkled like bright flames.

Her milky form and fairy hair shone like the sun
shimmering off the oceans of Mac Lir,
her pale lily skin reflected the torment
of the thorn reaching for the rose petal,
and I believed all she said.

Torn by love and confusion,
lost in a world too lost,
she sought peace and happiness,
but death hunted this
daughter of Tír na Nóg.

I followed her fair countenance,
while the crimson stain of her story
spread farther into the land,
and hoped the truth would be revealed,
yet powerless to break the spell.

One body, and then another
fell as if under the pikes of
the long dead heroes of '98,
and I feared she might be Niamh
come to bring me to Oisín.

She ran and I followed,
drawn by the need to hear
the end of her story, and
see the salvation of the rose
from the thorns of life.

We stopped
where the earth met heaven and hell.
The dead surrounded us,
and we stood before the cause of evil.
She pleaded for our freedom,

But her sweet words went unheeded.
The true sadness of the woman
revealed itself to me, and I saw
that love is fleeting like life and liberty.
I stood frozen beside the struggle

Apart, but not a part, my words
just a wisp of air, unheeded
by them both. As the struggle
raged, her hesitation vanished,
and when the blow of death came,

she threw herself over me.
Her act of sacrifice and bravery
freed her from the yoke of fear,
brought the sun into her life,
and saved us all.

The tale itself was done,
and on another clear morning
the woman left with her
new found treasure. The freedom
she had earned was hers to keep.

* * *